CHRIS FARNELL was born in Leicester in 1984. He's been making up stories as far back as he can remember and started writing *Mark II* when he should have been revising for his A Levels. He continued writing *Mark II* while he studied English Literature and Creative Writing at the University of East Anglia in Norwich – where he still lives, writes and works.

Mark II

Chris Farnell

**Tindal
Street
Press**

First published in April 2006 by
Tindal Street Press Ltd
217 The Custard Factory, Gibb Street, Birmingham, B9 4AA
www.tindalstreet.co.uk

A CIP catalogue reference for this book is available
from the British Library

ISBN 10:   0 9547913 9 8
ISBN 13:   978 0 9547913 9 1

Typeset by Country Setting, Kingsdown, Kent

Printed and bound in Great Britain by Clays Ltd, St Ives PLC

Clone

Clone

'You remember how Mark was very ill?' Lauren's mum said in the kind of forced cheerful voice she used when talking about things like death and Santa Claus.

'Mum, I'm ten years old, not ten days,' Lauren sighed.

Of course Lauren remembered when Mark was ill. It was only a couple of months since she'd sat at the side of his hospital bed while her mum talked and Mark stared out of the window. Mark had never looked healthy. When Lauren thought of him she remembered a thin pasty wreck wasting in bed with tubes up his nose, wearing a Man United shirt as if he was a wire coat hanger.

The weeks since Mark died had been confusing. It had been annoying, the way Mum and Dad had explained absolutely everything that happened. Lauren hadn't needed much explaining; she *knew* Mark had died, and that this meant he was going to heaven, although some people believed he'd been reincarnated or had gone to a different type of heaven, and this was perfectly all right because all religions were equally valid although the Christian Church in England was obviously the proper one. She also knew that it didn't matter if he didn't go to heaven, because a bit of him was always going to be with them in their hearts. Lauren didn't know *which* bit.

She didn't know why instead of feeling sad she felt numb most of the time. She didn't know why she'd be playing on the computer or doing some homework, feeling totally happy, and then remember that Mark wasn't alive any more, and suddenly feel guilty for forgetting. She hadn't bothered to ask her parents about those bits. Somehow she got the feeling that her parents were explaining everything to her precisely because they didn't know the answers themselves.

Her mum continued explaining. 'Well, Mark was ill because there was something wrong with his genes, which are like the blueprints for making a person . . .'

'Mark made us watch *Jurassic Park* three times, Mum. I know what DNA is,' Lauren pointed out.

'Anyway,' her mum said, 'we all loved Mark very much, didn't we?'

'Yes, Mum,' Lauren said. 'We've been through this.'

'Well, we thought it would be nice if we could bring him back, in a way,' her mum said. 'So we kept some of his magic blueprints . . .'

'You can say genetic material, Mum.'

'. . . and we found the parts that made Mark sick and took them out,' her mum continued, ignoring the interruption. 'Now the scientists are going to use those blueprints to make a new Mark who won't get sick, and then he can come and live with us and it will be just like the old Mark was here again.'

'You're bringing him back to life?'

'Not exactly. He'll be very much like Mark, and we'll treat him just like we treated Mark,' her mum said, 'but he might be slightly different.'

'But if he's not really Mark, why will we treat him just like Mark?' Lauren asked.

'Because he's . . . he's a new Mark. Just like the old one, but without the illness. But we'll still remember and love the old Mark as well . . .'

Again Lauren wondered whether her parents were in a position to explain anything.

It wasn't the first time I'd been to the Selfs' house. I'd been there every day since I'd started secondary school. I'd long passed the stage when I'd walk in and be hit by the sphere of politeness reserved for guests – the one made to create the illusion that the Selfs never had rows over where the car keys had gone or how Lauren spent her dinner money. By now the family treated me with the kind of indifference reserved for pieces of furniture and familiar school friends. Sometimes I reckon I could have walked into the bathroom while Mrs Self was in the shower and not heard anything more than a cursory 'Hi, Phil.'

Okay, I've called it the Selfs' house, but for me it was always Mark's house. Mrs Self had never been Mrs Self. She'd just been Mark's mum. I felt silly calling her Mrs Self as if she was a teacher, but calling her Angela didn't seem right either, so if I had to talk to her I avoided calling her anything.

I'd go there every morning because Mark's mum knew my dad, and Mark's mum was worried about Mark getting picked on if his mum took him to school, so I was given the task.

She needn't have worried. In high school they pick on you because you're shy, fat, short, skinny, tall, wear glasses, have ginger hair, have a speech impediment or speak posh. They make fun of you if you watch *Star Trek* or if you're football mad, they make fun of you if you're clever and they make fun of you if you're thick. They make fun of you just because they need someone to make fun of and you aren't smart or quick enough to make that someone somebody else. But they don't make fun of you for being disabled. It's not out of any kind of morality, no honour among bullies or anything like that. It's simply because teachers (who'd happily ignore most types of torture if they could finish their tea undisturbed) would come down like a ton of bricks on anybody who was seen as *discriminating* against anyone. Anyone meant Mark, the school's disabled kid, and Vivek, the school Asian.

Of course this just meant they never did it to his face. Everyone knew the Mark Self jokes that you'd hear circulating around the class when he wasn't there, just like everyone's heard Mike Reeve doing his Punjabi accent when Vivek isn't around. Even some of the teachers knew about it, but they're the ones who laugh at the jokes themselves – because they're scared of the class and would do anything to turn attention on to someone else, or because (and I've never been sure if this is really much worse) some teachers are as shitty as the brats they teach.

I'd been to the Selfs' house before, but today was different. It was the first time I'd been in Mark's house since the funeral. The funeral had been weird. I'd had to stop myself laughing; it had all seemed so funny. It was funny because everyone was acting so solemn, almost as if Mark had died. Of course, he had. That was the thing. His heartbeat had stopped and they'd put him in a wooden box and they were going to cremate him. But something about the idea still made me laugh and shake my head in disbelief, the way you do when you see parents shouting at small children who have no idea what's wrong with the word 'arsehole'.

You see, I'd never really believed he was dead. There was this massive sham funeral with lots of weepy parents. Even Lauren, Mark's sister, cried and looked, just for a moment, like a little girl instead of the brat monster from hell. Then I'd gone to school and it had seemed slightly odd that Mark wasn't in today.

Some mornings I'd ring the doorbell and stand humming while I waited for his mum to answer the door. Then her tear-streaked face would appear and the memory would come rushing up like a light bulb held under water and lodge itself firmly in my throat. I'd apologize and then run off to school.

When I arrived today I found the door left wide open and a lot of excited talking going on inside. I rang the doorbell anyway and Mark's mum poked her head round from the kitchen, a weird smile on her face.

'Phil!' she said cheerfully. 'Come in! Mark's back!'

She said it as if Mark had returned from America after going to seek his fortune, but I knew what she meant. I'd been told all about the new cloning techniques over the phone, the Kwik-Learn system they'd developed to help people with amnesia, how the new Mark would look, act and maybe even think the same way as the old one.

I stepped into the living room, full of other people's house things: ornaments that might or might not have held sentimental value, photographs of family holidays and Christmases that seemed like freakish reflections of my own. It was all familiar stuff; all things I'd stared at with mild curiosity while Mark's mum helped him with his shoes every morning.

The first person I saw was Lauren, kneeling by the settee with her chin on her arms, watching Mark with a look of unashamed malevolence. Then there was Mark's dad, sat next to him and holding a tissue to Mark's nose. I couldn't tell you what was going on in his mind: Mark's dad was the type to keep his opinions to himself.

Then I looked at Mark, and it was only when I saw him sitting there in his Man United shirt, clutching his bloodied nose and looking around the room in much the same way I used to, that I realized Mark Self was dead.

I never believed you could tell anything from someone's eyes. I'd dissected a pig's eye in biology and looking at it sitting on the Petri dish staring up at me, I had been unable to tell if it had met its demise with shock, or with a knowledge that the inevitable had arrived, or with relief that the endlessly tedious life of pigdom was finally over. It was, after all, just a small blob of organic matter that absorbed light and then sent electrical impulses into the brain.

So the only way I can explain what I saw in Mark's eyes that day is that somehow my subconscious gathered up all the information it had picked up elsewhere, and tricked me into thinking that it was Mark's eyes telling me all that they did.

Sure, Mark looked different. A healthy amount of fat and muscle covered his arms and neck, as if someone had taken a wire-frame model and filled in the gaps with Plasticine. He was sitting upright now instead of just slumping like he used to, and his nose was bleeding. Mark had never suffered so much as a scratch in all the time I'd known him. But all of this could simply have been a sign he'd got over his illness.

But his eyes, they looked . . . the only word I can think of is babyish. They were wide open and constantly changing direction. They rested slightly longer on his dad and sister than elsewhere, but then they were off again, looking at the photos and ornaments with intense fascination.

Nobody ever looked that fascinated in their own living room.

Mark's mum came in, smiling anxiously.

'Say hello to Phil,' she said.

Mark – that is, Mark's clone – looked at me with those wide baby eyes. I had to stop myself jerking back when I saw the recognition in them.

He said, 'Hello, Phil. You're my best friend, aren't you?'

I shrugged. 'Um, yeah, I suppose.'

We stayed like that: me, Mark's clone, mum, dad and sister. Eventually Mark's mum's smile renewed itself.

'Brian? Lauren? Why don't we leave the boys to get re-acquainted?' Mark's dad and sister left obediently. I bit my lip. Lauren had never left a room obediently in her life.

Mark's mum didn't notice, or pretended not to. She turned to Mark.

'Do you like biscuits? Of course you like biscuits, you've always liked biscuits. I'll go and get some biscuits . . .'

I sat down on the settee next to Mark.

'How'd you get the nosebleed?' I asked.

'Oh, you know, me, three thugs and some advanced martial arts. They came off worse.'

I shook my head. Mark hadn't said that. Not Mark's clone anyway. It was the mini-Mark I kept in my head, the one who acted exactly as I expected and wanted. I suppose in a way you could call him Mark's ghost.

The Mark clone put his hand up to his face as if he'd only just noticed it was there.

'Me and my dad went outside to play football,' Mark said. 'I don't think I was very good.'

I tensed up. It was like Mark was doing a really good impression of a four-year-old.

'You like football?' I asked.

'Yeah, I love football,' Mark said without conviction. 'I couldn't play it when I was ill but I used to go to all the games. Dad's got a season ticket for Manchester United, so we can go and watch them play.'

Now he sounded like a four-year-old doing a really good impression of Mark. He'd obviously been told that he used to go to matches before – before what? Before he existed? I knew Mark was dead now, but there was something eerie about this clone. He'd *recognized* me. He'd looked at me with Mark's face and he'd known straightaway who I was. That didn't feel right – it didn't feel right at all.

'Listen . . . Mark,' I said, leaning forward, 'there's something you should know about you and football –'

'Biscuits!' Mark's mum said, coming in with a plate.

She placed them on the glass coffee table and watched intently as Mark went to pick one. There were three types of biscuit on the plate: Chocolate Hobnob, Custard Cream and Ginger Nut. Mark had loved Chocolate Hobnobs.

The clone's hand hovered over the plate, and as it moved Mark's mum's eyes went with it. It went over the Hobnobs, over the Custard Creams, over the Ginger Nuts, back over the Custard Creams, back to the Ginger Nuts . . .

'Do you want a Chocolate Hobnob, Mark?' she asked. 'They always were . . . they're your favourite!'

Mark picked up a Chocolate Hobnob and bit into it thoughtfully.

'Phil, could you come and help me bring the drinks in?' Mark's mum asked.

I got up and followed her into the kitchen.

'Well?' she asked.

I looked at her dumbly, then said, 'He's very nice.'

'Isn't he just like Mark?' she asked. 'He even recognizes

everyone and knows his way around the house! I mean, I know they taught him all those things at the hospital with that speed learning, but you never know. I mean, you hear things about genetic memory and such, don't you? You saw the way he kept looking around the room as if it was familiar, didn't you?'

I should have told her there and then. I should have told her that her son, her firstborn son and my best friend, was dead. I consoled myself afterwards by saying hundreds of professionals must have already tried to tell her, that no matter how plainly you said it she would never have listened because she wanted her little boy back. I told myself that, and maybe it was even true, but that wasn't the real reason I kept quiet. The truth is I chickened out. I like to think I'm grown up. In two and a bit years I'll be allowed to have sex and even a cigarette afterwards, in three I can drive and in four I can drink. But the truth is, essentially I'm still a kid. I was smart enough to see that Mark's mum, Angela, was turning to me for help, and at nearly fourteen having a grown-up turn to you for help with anything more complicated than the household chores can scare the hell out of you.

'Yeah, I think I know what you mean,' I muttered, without making eye contact.

We took the glasses and a bottle of pop into the living room.

'Well, I'll leave you two to it,' Mark's mum said, smiling, always smiling.

'Actually, do you know where the bathroom is?' I asked.

No idea why I asked. I suppose it was because my best friend didn't live here any more, and somehow I felt that changed the geography.

'Up the stairs, turn left and it's straight in front of you,' Mark's clone said.

Even Mark's mum stared this time.

'Right, thanks, Mark,' I said.

'Why didn't you know already?' the clone asked. 'You've been here hundreds of times.'

I stood open-mouthed for a second, before spluttering, 'I'm sorry, but I really need to pee!' and running up the stairs.

Once the bathroom door was locked I sighed and slid down it to the floor. Opening the door seemed like the worst thing in the world right now. I crouched with my back against it, clutching my head and shaking.

I stood up and went over to the mirror, looked at my face and was suddenly overcome with the absurdity of it all. Faces, they're just a convenient space to put all the organs we use for finding out about the world. Everyone has them: people, monkeys, fish, lizards; even squid have something that looks vaguely facial. We see faces where there aren't any, in the clouds, on the front of cars, hell, even in sodding pizzas. Why do people put so much importance on them? Why is something true if you can say it looking into somebody's eyes? If you are well known you become 'a face'. If you act one way with one person and differently with someone else you are 'two faced'. Your face is who you are.

Seeing Mark's face and knowing, just *knowing* that it wasn't him, it freaked me out. I splashed some water on my face and dried it off before opening the door. I held my breath before unlocking the latch, like I was stepping on to a stage, or into an arena.

When I stepped out on to the landing I caught a glimpse of Lauren sprawled out on her bed in the next room. She was playing on a GameBoy – not one of the credit-card sized colour ones you get now, but one of the original house-brick affairs that Mark had been bought when he was little.

'Hi,' I said as I reached the door.

Without meaning to, I stopped and stood by the door, watching Lauren.

She glared up at me with the look of withering contempt that was her way of saying hello.

'Hiya, Fart-face,' she said, and turned back to her game.

I didn't move from the door.

'Your brother's gonna go nuts if he finds you nicked his GameBoy,' I said, leaning against the doorframe.

'That's not my brother,' Lauren said.

She didn't sound angry, or upset, or as if she was about to have some ten-year-old sulk. It was a statement, something she'd realized and accepted, if not actually liked.

Right then, I wanted more than anything to run over and give Lauren a hug.

'What makes you say that?' I asked without moving.

'You mean you can't tell?' she said in astonishment. 'He's too nice. He says please and thank you, and he hasn't called me a rude name since he got here.'

I frowned. I knew as much as anyone that the impostor downstairs wasn't my best friend, but I didn't like hearing someone talk about him like this.

'Mark was nice,' I protested.

'Yeah,' Lauren admitted, 'but he was always nice in a nasty way . . . or nasty in a nice way. Do you know what I mean? And he always used to go into sulks whenever I was playing with Dad or when we went swimming and he had to sit on the side.'

I nodded at this. Mark always hated the exclusion the illness brought about more than anything. At the school disco we'd sit in the corner drinking Panda Pops and I could see Mark staring out on to the dance floor with real bitterness. Sometimes I'd even resented him, keeping me on the sidelines with him so that he wouldn't feel alone. Sadly, Mark couldn't keep me from PE, but when I came back from rugby lessons he'd be sitting there looking at me with envy and resentment, so that I didn't dare open my mouth to complain about having Chaz Spencer elbow drop me for trying to pick up the ball.

'Do you think he's Mark?' Lauren asked.

I looked at her. She wasn't like her mum. She wasn't asking me for help. She was simply trying to prove a point, if only to herself.

I sighed. Now that I was upstairs and had been given time to recover, the possibility didn't seem so ridiculous. Maybe my initial reaction had simply been down to shock. After all, he *was* supposed to be dead, and here he was. All that stuff his mum had said about genetic memory, was it really so far-fetched? We don't know what information is stored in our genes, do we?

'I don't know,' I answered, and left.

When I got to the bottom of the stairs, I did, straight away. As soon as I saw the clone sitting there, gazing round the room, I realized all over again that this was not the person I'd been going to school with for the last three years.

'Hello,' the clone said, staring at me.

It was a completely passive stare – the stare of a baby who's seen something it's recognized and has decided to focus on, like a rattle or a teddy bear.

'Hi,' I said tonelessly.

'Oh, by the way, Phil,' Mark's mum asked, 'will you still be coming over tomorrow to meet Mark for school?'

'Well, he doesn't need me to, does he? He can walk. He knows the way,' I said. I hadn't meant it to sound cruel, but I think it came out that way.

'Yes, but he's never actually been to school on his own, has he?' Mark's mum said.

I could have imagined the pause between 'school' and 'on' – I could have. She was looking at me in that helpless way again.

'Okay, I'll come round tomorrow,' I said. 'But I have to go now. My dad'll be expecting me back.'

'Goodbye, Phil,' Mark's clone said as I reached the door.

'Bye . . . Mark,' I said, without looking back.

When I closed the front door it felt like coming up for air.

Lauren sat up in bed, propped against the wall with her eyes locked on the TV screen. She was still in her old bedroom. When the new brother had first arrived she'd suggested that, since she was technically the oldest now, she should have the big bedroom downstairs – the one that had traditionally been Mark's. This had made her mum get very cross. She'd said that Mark was still her big brother and she should treat him with the respect she'd always done.

Lauren had been shocked – she'd *never* treated her big brother with respect.

The reason she was awake now, at half past eleven on a

Sunday night, was that Kate from school had told her there was a good horror film on tonight. It was called *Invasion of the Body Snatchers* and it sounded really gory. Lauren had worked hard to stay up this late, sneaking down to the kitchen a couple of times when her parents had gone to bed and stealing Sunny D, reading, listening to loud music (with her headphones on, of course). At one point she'd nearly dropped off, when the ten o'clock news had magically transformed into a nostalgic rockumentary in the blink of an eye. Now the film was about to start at last and Lauren was wide awake, or at least in a sitting position that would be impossible to sleep in.

'And now on BBC One, whatever you do, don't fall asleep . . .' the voice-over said to the background of a modern dance performance in a scrapyard.

Lauren groaned when she realized the film was in black and white. She lay down in bed, deciding it had definitely not been worth staying up for – but she didn't turn the telly off. She was just about ready to drift off to sleep when something caught her attention.

She sat bolt upright. A young boy was crying, claiming that his aunt who looked after him wasn't really his aunt. She looked and acted exactly like his aunt, but the little boy just knew it wasn't the same person. Lauren watched attentively until the end credits rolled.

One by one people were replaced by these alien vegetables who landed in your back garden, and then gradually took on your shape before killing you and taking your place in your sleep. Soon the town was filled with aliens who looked and talked like the normal people they'd replaced and remembered everything exactly the same way. The only difference was that these ones were intent on taking over the world.

Lauren turned the telly off and lay curled up in bed, terrified of falling asleep. When she woke up the next day she was relieved to find that she wasn't a pod person. Then she saw Mark.

That night I lay awake in bed thinking about Mark. I remembered all the times I'd been over to his house and his parents would ask me how I was doing in school, and every time I'd smile and say, 'It's going okay. I only wish I was as hard working as Mark here.'

It was a lie, and an obvious one, my way of calling the Fifth Amendment. Mark got bored easily and tended to space out in class. I did well at school not because I grafted any harder, but because I genuinely found the work interesting and could get stuck in for hours without even noticing it. Of course, Mark's parents would have loved nothing more than to ask, 'Why can't you work as hard as Phil?' or 'Maybe Phil could help you with your homework?' and neither of us wanted that.

Okay, so far I've painted a pretty bad picture of Mark. You might even wonder why he was my best friend. He did enjoy his self-pity, and he wasn't one of those heroic Channel Five TV movie kids whose feisty personality allowed him to grow beyond his disability. Mark hated being ill all the time; he was jealous of all those healthy people going off and enjoying their lives. When I stayed the night at his house he'd lie in bed moaning about wanting a normal life until I was sick of hearing about it.

But that wasn't all there was to him. Somehow, maybe not even out of choice, I'd come to rely on Mark. He had a knack: no matter how serious a situation, no matter how depressed you might be feeling, he could say just the right thing and turn lead into whipped cream. He'd make some wisecrack and suddenly problems wouldn't seem quite so important any more. It wasn't just that he trivialized things, though. Something about the way he smiled when he spoke made you think he understood and sympathized. Neither of us wanted a deep meaningful discussion about whatever the situation was, so we just shared quips and understanding.

I'd never said it out loud, but I loved Mark, and that night I found myself wondering if he knew that. The thing was, we'd never said a lot of things outright – so much of it rested on some mystical 'understanding'. Even when he'd been in the hospital and it was clear that he wouldn't pull through, I'd never truly realized it. I'd sit by his bed and he'd moan about the food, and I'd talk about how shitty school was, we'd trade insults and I'd sneak in chips and the latest *FHM*.

At night we'd trade text messages. Stuff like a list of brackets and full stops that formed the image of a monkey's face, followed by 'Hey look! UR mobile has a mirror!' or 'Uve got wit Uve got charm Uve got sex appeal – shit Ive got the wrong number!' Hilarious, huh?

Then one day I got a text saying, 'Remember – no matter wut, Uve got to strut.' I sent him a reply saying, 'WTF R U on?' and there was no reply. Later I sent him one saying, 'Roses R Red, Violets R Blue, Poo smells of Shit, and so do U.' Not even a simple 'Fuck U' in reply. I was worried; Mark was starting to forget even common courtesy.

The next day his mum made the ludicrous statement that he was dead.

Something I never quite figured out – according to my phone, that last text message was sent a full half hour after Mark was dead. The network must have been down or something.

Memories turned into dreams. I turned up to the SATs stark naked. I relived my sixth birthday party, the one where me and some friends had gone to a fast-food restaurant and I'd been brutally savaged by a clown. I stood at the top of a staircase being chased by clockwork vampires but couldn't run away. They weren't exactly separate dreams; it was like one of those surreal pop videos where one scene merges seamlessly and unreasoningly into the next. Throughout all of them I could see Mark, just sitting in the background in his wheelchair, watching me.

My first thought when I woke up, that is my first actual thought, rather than the slow realization that I was conscious, was 'Oh, he's dead.' It wasn't fuelled by any particular emotion. At the time I felt more strongly about my second thought, which was 'Oh, it's Monday.'

That was half seven. At ten past eight I leapt out of bed, pulled the least crumpled set of clothes off the floor and dashed out the door, only coming back for my schoolbag.

Once I was out of the house my feet went into autopilot. I was oblivious to the paperboy, the corner shop, the smell of manure wafting in from outside the village. The Monday morning school journey was a dead zone for conscious thought. My mind was like a treasure chest filled with cold, lumpy porridge. Occasionally the jewel of a thought would float to the surface, but it would be submerged by oaty goodness before you could catch it.

One of these gems was, 'Do I really have to go and pick

the clone up?' After all, I reasoned, I didn't have any kind of obligation to it. It just happened to look like my dead best friend – so what? My gran looked a bit like the queen but that didn't give her the divine right to rule. Of course, it being early on a Monday morning I then went on to wonder if a clone of Queen Elizabeth would actually be more entitled to the throne than Prince Charles, since the heir is supposed to be the closest living relative and you can't get much closer than your own clone. However, I soon stumbled back on to my original train of thought. I supposed that I did have a sort of obligation to Mark's family. He'd never actually made me promise anything soppy like 'look after my family', but if one of us couldn't do something the other always jumped in to do it instead, like Mark's maths homework.

This was ridiculous, another chunk of my mind argued. I didn't even *like* the clone. It just sat there staring around like a confused rhesus monkey, occasionally spouting the odd line of phrasebook English. Besides, why should I help Mark's family on his behalf if his family were so quick to replace him? I was pretty sure Mark wouldn't have liked his clone one bit.

After deciding finally, once and for all, that I was definitely not going to pick up the clone, I discovered that force of habit had guided me to the Selfs' front door again and I was standing in front of the scowling figure of Mark's little sister.

'Come in,' she said. 'Mark's in his room getting his shoes on.'

The word 'Mark' had a just noticeable edge to it. The edge Lauren used when she called relatives she didn't like 'sir' or 'ma'am'. Anyone who didn't know her would have missed it, but it was there.

'By himself?' I asked in amazement.

'Uh huh,' she answered, and disappeared upstairs.

I wandered over to Mark's room to find his mum shyly orbiting the clone as it put its shoes on. No parent would ever claim they *wanted* their kids to be disabled, but I could see Mark's mum was having real trouble stopping herself from leaping forward and putting the clone's shoes on for it.

'Hiya,' I said from the hallway.

'Oh, hello, Phil,' she said.

'Hello, Phil,' the clone said, standing up and looking at me.

It was freaky. Now I saw it standing up in school uniform, I was more aware than ever of two things – that it did look exactly like Mark Self, and that it really wasn't Mark Self.

When we were safely out the front door, I realized that this was the first time I'd been with the clone out of earshot of Mark's parents.

'Okay, this is all wrong,' I said, stopping it. 'First, take your shirt out of your trousers.'

The clone looked confused. 'Why? I thought the school rules said that you had to keep your shirt tucked in.'

'Yeah, but it makes you look like a geek,' I said.

'Why?'

'Because . . . because it's a pointless school rule and nobody obeys it. So if you do obey it you'll stand out a mile,' I explained.

'Oh,' the clone said, and carefully pulled its shirt out of its trousers.

'Right. Next, tuck your tie into the top of your shirt.'

'Why?'

'Same reason as the shirt. Do it,' I persisted.

I stood back. At least it looked halfway presentable now. In fact it looked a lot more like Mark would've looked if he had ever stood up. I tried to forget that bit.

'That's better. Come on, you freak, let's see if we can get into school before lunch.'

'Freak?' the clone asked.

'What about it?' I said.

'Strange, bizarre, deformed, am I those things?' the clone said.

It wasn't being defensive. It wasn't even insulted. It was asking in the spirit of honest curiosity.

'Well, no, not really,' I said, deciding that I didn't want to trigger a conversation with Mark's mum.

'Then why did you call me one?' the clone asked.

Again there was no hint that it was arguing a point, it was just asking questions.

'Well, it's just, you know . . .'

'No.'

'It's like an insult, it doesn't mean anything,' I said, shrugging.

'Why are you insulting me? I thought you were my best friend,' the clone said.

During the conversation I found myself gradually avoiding eye contact and speaking more quietly, the way you used to when you were little and in for a particularly harsh bollocking. Which was stupid because I wasn't in for a bollocking at all. This was closer to the talk on How Babies Are Made.

'I dunno,' I said, shrugging again. 'Friends do that, insult each other and stuff. It's just the way people are.'

'Why?'

'I suppose, um, when you get to know someone well enough, and you trust them enough, you can hurl abuse at each other and know it doesn't mean anything, so it doesn't matter.'

'I see,' the clone said. 'You insult people to show that you can insult them without it really mattering, because they know you're lying?'

'Lying?'

'You said that I wasn't really a freak,' the clone said.

I took a deep breath. 'Yes, you've got it exactly right.'

'Oh,' the clone said thoughtfully, then added, 'dick wad.'

I frowned at the back of the clone's head as it walked on. I was sure it hadn't learned words like that at home.

When we got to school I quickened the pace and hoped the clone would have the sense to keep up. He didn't. Instead, the clone stopped at the gateposts and stared at the school. He smiled, the poor sod actually smiled. During whatever conditioning or memory enhancement they did in the lab, the cruel bastards had made the clone think he liked school. I shook my head in despair. *That* was a travesty of nature.

I looked back at the building to see if I could make sense of the glee and wonderment on the clone's face. I couldn't. It was just your usual dull suburban secondary school that might have looked modern thirty years ago. It hadn't changed much since then, except for an increasingly high fence around the grounds to prevent a perfectly understandable truancy problem.

'Oi! Phil!'

I cursed under my breath, grabbed the clone by the arm and dragged him along after me.

'Phil! Don't ignore me, you shit!'

'I think they want to talk to you,' the clone said, tugging at my arm.

'Off for a smooch behind the art block?' Chaz said, catching us up.

He did a double take of the clone.

'Hey, I thought you were dead?' he said.

'It's okay. I'm not any more,' the clone said. Then, after thinking for a second, it added, 'You moron.'

I wanted to curl up in a ball.

'What did you just call me?' Chaz asked, squaring up.

'A moron,' the clone said. 'Is that a problem?'

I wanted to dig a hole, climb in and cave in the entrance. The clone hadn't been getting confrontational; it honestly wanted to know if it was a problem. Chaz didn't pick up on that. He wasn't the perceptive type. Every school has a Chaz: the big thick kid with lots of small thick friends, who finds nothing funnier than seeing somebody scared. His hobbies were detention and sneaking out to the fields to smoke. He wasn't old enough to drink, but his every word sounded like you'd just knocked over his beer. His head was shaved, his forehead was sloping, he even had a scar across one eyebrow. He was the thirteen-year-old incarnation of evil.

'Yes, it's a problem,' Chaz said, giving the clone a quiet shove. 'Your problem. Now are you going to apologize, or am I going to have to kick the crap out of you?'

'I'll apologize,' the clone said. 'I'm sorry.'

Chaz frowned. 'Didn't sound like you *really* meant it,' he said. 'I'm going to have to kick your head in anyway . . .'

'Wait a second!' I said, stepping in.

God help me, I stepped in. Okay, I was kind of obliged to: I felt at least partly responsible for the clone calling Chaz a moron. Plus, well, the clone really did look a lot like Mark. I mean, in a way it was Mark, wasn't it? It had Mark's DNA, Mark's face, voice and hair, Mark's name. It was Mark in every way except the ways that mattered. Unfortunately that was enough to make me stand in front of Chaz Spencer.

'Out of the way,' Chaz said.

'Look, this is all a really, really bad misunderstanding. Mark here was just having a bit of a joke, you see, sorry, it wasn't meant personally or anything,' I said quickly.

Chaz paused. A look of painful concentration passed over his face.

'Are you really Mark?' he asked, looking past me.

'Yes,' the clone said.

In the short time I'd known the clone it had switched between two emotional states, indifference and curiosity. I'd never heard it say anything with any conviction, but that one word had power. The clone had said it in the same tone of voice as action heroes who've been told they'll never get out alive, or mad scientists who've been asked if their insane schemes could possibly work. It was the kind of voice that made disagreeing seem absurd.

'No way,' Chaz sneered. 'You can't be. Where's your chair?'

Other people were starting to notice us and coming over to look. I felt my ears go red. I'd much rather Chaz had simply kicked the shit out of the pair of us and left us in a bleeding heap.

'I don't need it,' the clone said.

Chaz stepped past me and gave the clone another shove. Mark and Chaz had never been good friends. Mark knew Chaz couldn't lay a finger on him and so he'd put the boot in whenever he got the chance.

The clone didn't know this.

'Well, I hope you still have it around,' Chaz said, cracking his knuckles. 'You'll be needing it.'

25

He squared up to Mark again. I did the only thing I could: I lowered my head and charged at Chaz – hitting him in the chest and knocking him back a good three feet before he got hold of me and the pain began.

The thing about playground fights is they're vicious. I clawed at Chaz, desperately searching for something soft to dig my fingers into; he grabbed my head and kneed me in the face. As we fought we started to spin; we span faster and faster in the hope that one of us would lose his footing. The thing about playground fights is they're merciless. If me or Chaz had recoiled in pain, or paused to catch our breath, the other would have come in even harder than before, trying to squeeze the last of the fight out of him.

The thing about playground fights is they're crap. For all the punching, kicking, eye-gouging fun, they look shit; none of that *Matrix* stuff, no *Buffy*-esque martial arts, not even the equivalent of a good movie fist-fight. As me and Chaz were locked in a bloodthirsty struggle, to the clone and the rest of the school it must have looked like we were having a bit of a hug.

In my defence I'd like to say I punched him pretty hard in the coat a couple of times and did a good job head-butting his Doc Martens. Eventually the chant of 'Fight! Fight! Fight!' summoned a teacher. As soon as Mr Briggs was close enough, I leapt away, looking dazed and shocked as he struggled to hold Chaz back. At one point Chaz fought past him and planted one on the side of my head, but soon I was safely ensconced in the medical room.

Chaz claimed that I'd attacked him unprovoked, but Mr Briggs decided to implement a 'no blame' approach, where we both shook hands and said sorry. Mr Briggs pretended not to notice when Chaz's grip practically crushed my fingers.

We got out of the medical room after being told letters would be sent home, and the school wouldn't stand for this kind of behaviour. By then it was lunchtime, and I had no idea where Mark – that is, the clone – had got to.

I wandered the corridors searching for him, occasionally having to hide between the lockers when a dinner lady walked past. It was freezing outside, but unless it was actually raining frogs all pupils were forced to stay out on the playground during breaks. The only exceptions to the rule were those lucky people who had somehow wangled a library pass. Usually Mark and I were among this small elite thanks to Mark's wheelchair.

I found the clone standing outside the library arguing with one of the dinner ladies. (The teachers tried to make us call them 'lunchtime supervisors' and we ignored them.)

'But I always come in here at lunchtime,' the clone was saying.

'Maybe, but if you haven't got a pass you aren't going in. Now come on, get out to the playground. The fresh air will do you good,' the dinner lady said firmly.

'Hey, Mark!' I shouted, running up to meet him.

It was only afterwards I realized how natural it had sounded and cursed myself. That replica was *not* Mark, I kept reminding myself.

'Hi, Phil,' the clone said, turning round and waving. 'Are you okay?'

'Yeah, nothing major surgery can't fix,' I said.

'Major surgery?' Mark asked. 'That sounds quite serious. I thought you'd be in hospital if it was that bad.'

'A joke, it was a joke,' I reassured it. 'What are you doing?'

'The lunchtime supervisor won't let me into the library,' Mark said.

'Oh well, who wants to read a load of books anyway?' I said, leading it away. 'Besides, I've not had lunch yet.'

I was going to take the clone to the dinner hall, but I remembered that would mean everyone staring at us again. Better to go hungry. So I took it behind the art block instead, an unsupervised bit of playground that hadn't been discovered by the smokers yet.

'So, how was your morning?' I asked.

'It was . . . interesting,' Mark said, sitting on a wall.

'Interesting?'

'A lot of people didn't think I was Mark. They kept whispering things and looking at me in a funny way,' Mark said, as if he were describing the homework Mr Jones had set.

'Well, you're bound to get a lot of that,' I said. 'It's a bit weird for everyone.'

We sat in silence for a bit. I couldn't tell him. I couldn't point out that he was a cheap copy of a real person. I couldn't explain why for most of us, me more than anyone, it was as impossible to accept him as Mark as it was to grasp that Mark was dead.

'Phil?' the clone said suddenly.

'Yes?'

'What was I like before . . . you know, before?'

'Before what, Mark?' I wanted to ask. 'Just who do you think you are?'

Instead, I said, 'I dunno, really.'

'You must know. You were my best friend, weren't you?'

'Yeah, but . . .'

I didn't have a clue where to start. How the hell do you describe a person? Take the whole reality of someone's personality, memories, habits, anxieties, the petty arguments and the times when you'd found yourself depending on them and vice versa – how can you take all that and turn it into nothing but words? It just doesn't work.

Okay, what was the first thing I thought of when I thought of Mark?

'He was bitter,' I said, almost without thinking. 'He was bitter because he'd been thrown into life with all the dreams that everyone else had, but he couldn't make them come true. It pissed him off. It kinda twisted him; everything he said had this edge to it . . . but no, I mean, that wasn't all . . .'

I took a deep breath and said, 'I mean, he could be sarcastic and mean and he always knew just what to say to get at you, but . . . but he was my best mate. I didn't even know why half the time, but he was, and that matters, okay?'

'You mean I was your best mate,' the clone said.

I wasn't going to answer that one.

'You really liked me, didn't you?' the clone said.

I looked at him. 'What makes you say that?'

It was true, I did like him, I liked him more than anyone, but how anybody could get that from what I'd just said was beyond me.

'Well,' the clone said, 'when I asked my parents, or the other people in my class, or the teachers, they all said I was "nice" or I "had a great sense of humour". But you, you started talking about all the stuff that was wrong with me, but your voice sounded as if you were saying I had a great sense of humour. It was like you liked me *because* of all the things that were wrong with me, rather than ignoring them.'

It was then that I realized something of earth-shattering importance. The clone wasn't stupid. I wasn't lying when I said the clone was like a baby, but there's nothing stupid about a baby. The only important difference between the mind of a baby and the mind of a grown-up is that the baby hasn't learned all the rules yet. When the clone called Chaz a moron, that might have seemed like a stupid thing to do, but to the clone it must have seemed the right thing to say. He'd learned from me that friends insult each other as part of normal conversation. His parents had the strange belief that whenever two children of the same age met they'd automatically get on. They hadn't given the clone a list of classmates but a list of *friends*.

The clone wasn't stupid, but he didn't know the rules, and I had a horrible feeling I knew who'd be teaching him.

That night, dinner was butter-cooked chicken, roast potatoes and salad. Lauren watched the clone as he carefully cut each piece of chicken or potato into a bite-sized chunk, placed it in his mouth, chewed and swallowed. It was sickening. Mark had eaten like a pig – you'd have thought the clone could at least get that right.

Mum and Dad weren't paying any attention. They were too busy looking closely at their own dinners.

When everyone sat down Dad had asked Mark how his first day at school went. Mum quietly reminded him that it *wasn't* Mark's first day, and since then everyone had been eating in silence.

'Kate's going to Disney World next week,' Lauren said, just to break the silence.

'I thought I told you not to play with that girl?' her mum said.

'Wasn't playing,' Lauren said. 'We were just talking. Nothing wrong with talking, is there?'

'You know what I meant,' her mum said. 'She's not safe. I caught her playing in the road the other day. I could have run her over.'

'Yeah, well, she gets better holidays than us. Remember that dump we went to last year?' Lauren asked.

The noises of chewing and cutting stopped around the table. Everyone was looking at Mark.

'We went to Devon,' Mark said. 'We stayed in a caravan near the beach.'

Lauren heard her mum start breathing again.

'Really?' Lauren said. 'What colour was the caravan?'

'It was brown.'

Lauren nodded. Nobody had started eating again yet.

'One other thing,' she said. 'Did you like our bedroom there?'

Mark's forehead creased. He put his knife and fork down next to his plate.

'Did I like the bedroom?'

'Get on with your dinner, Lauren.'

'But Mum, I'm only asking . . .'

'Do as your mother says,' her dad said.

Lauren got her knife and cut a piece of chicken, making sure the knife scraped along the plate. While she ate, she wore her sulkiest expression.

It wasn't that she was trying to prove the clone wasn't her brother; she knew he wasn't. Nor was she trying to make her parents see that; the clone could be bright green and they'd still call it Mark. What she wanted to do was find out exactly what had taken her brother's place.

Before she went to bed Lauren snuck past Mark's bedroom and heard her parents laughing and talking inside. She peeked through a crack in the door and saw the clone with his back to her, staring at the TV. He was watching the video of their summer holiday last year.

'Yo bitch,' the clone said when he opened the door next morning.

'Yo bitch?' I asked.

'Yeah motherfu—'

'Hold on, let's go back to the *Yo bitch*,' I said. 'What's with the swearing?'

'I've been getting an edge to everything I say,' Mark said.

'I think you've got it a bit wrong,' I said as we started walking. 'Mark never used to swear – well, not much. Well, okay, quite a lot, but not like that. He was just a bit sarcastic sometimes.'

Mark thought for a second, then said, 'Yeah, and I knew that on account of being a mind reader!'

For a moment I couldn't speak. He'd sounded not quite like Mark, but close enough to spook me.

'Phil?' Mark said, in what I'd come to think of as his 'normal' voice.

'Yeah?'

'Why do people act weird in home videos?'

'What?'

'In home videos, everybody's always smiling and laughing and pulling silly faces, and they're always doing fun stuff like opening presents or playing games or getting married. Since I've moved back home all anyone does is cook meals, load the dishwasher and watch telly.'

'I think people just record important occasions, like weddings and birthdays and stuff,' I said.

'Why?'

'Well, they're nice things that they want to remember.'

'But wouldn't people want to remember what their ordinary days were like as well?'

'Nah, that's just boring.'

'Yeah, but if most of the days were like that, wouldn't people want to remember things as they really were? Rather than just picking out the nice bits? Otherwise they might get confused and think that in the past everything was all weddings and opening presents and that somehow everything's got worse so that now they only have dull boring days . . .' Mark said.

'How old are you?' I asked.

'Thirteen,' Mark said immediately.

'No, I mean how long have *you* been . . .' I began, before seeing the look Mark was giving me.

We walked the rest of the way to school in silence. Mark didn't seem to mind. He acted as if silence was just something that happened when people didn't have anything to say.

As we went through the school gates again, there was a mixed reaction. The seventh and eighth years didn't have a clue who we were and ignored us. The people in our year avoided us, but never went too far away. They hung a safe distance from us and tried to pretend they weren't staring.

It might've been because of the fight the day before, but

I didn't think so. I don't know what they were afraid of – if anything, the clone was less scary than his counterpart – but there was a space around us as we walked through the playground.

When we got to the lockers we ran into Kirsty. Kirsty was a pretty nice person in a way. She was some sort of die-hard Christian and took the whole Good Samaritan thing too seriously. Before Mark died she was always offering to help, opening doors for us and fetching paper and worksheets for him in class. Mark wasn't the slightest bit grateful. In fact he got pretty nasty about it at times. He called her 'the interfering cow'. I'd tease him sometimes, telling him she obviously had the hots for him. 'Nah,' he'd respond, 'she wouldn't dream of fraternizing with one of her projects.'

There was some truth in that. You got the feeling sometimes that the whole point in her being nice was to show you how nice she was. She'd say things like, 'Look, Mark, if things are, you know, ever really getting you down, if there's anything I can do, you only have to ask. I really mean it,' and Mark would reply with something withering.

Mark treated her like shit, although I won't deny I could see his point (straight after Mark died she'd tried the same thing on me). But I couldn't help feeling a little sorry for her. The weird thing was that no matter how venomous he was, no matter how barbed his comments and no matter how often he responded to a cheerful hello with just a grunt and an evil expression, she never stopped being friendly. Mark would say it was because she couldn't take a hint if it ran her over, but I wasn't so sure.

'She's a friend, isn't she?' Mark said as we arrived at the lockers.

At least he'd learned his lesson from Chaz.

'Ummm . . . yeah, kind of,' I said.

'Hi, Kirsty,' Mark said, offering a handshake. A handshake!

Kirsty looked as if Mark had slapped her. In all the time I'd known her, she'd taken Mark's barrage of insults with a martyr-like smile. When Mark was really laying it on, that smile might become a little stiff, but it never broke.

Now she just went pale. Then she crammed her books into her bag as quickly as possible and pushed past us without making eye contact.

Mark looked confused. 'What's her problem?' he asked.

I suppose it was meant to sound bitchy and sarcastic. Unfortunately Mark still hadn't got the hang of that so it came out in his usual tone of polite enquiry.

'No idea,' I said, watching her flee down the corridor.

The first lesson I shared with Mark was maths, just before lunch. I enjoy maths; it's always so much easier than real life. You just have to move that number to here, that decimal point to there, factor those numbers and hey presto, that's what X is. Except today it wasn't like that.

X wasn't a number; it was made up of lots of other unknown quantities like Y and Z. You couldn't really find an answer to the problem, only put it differently. Next to me Mark didn't seem to mind. He readily accepted the letters as another form of number and sped through the questions.

It wasn't long before he was at the front of the class asking for the next sheet. Mrs Shelley passed it to him at arm's length. It turned out the teachers didn't like the clone any more than the pupils did. They would answer his questions in the quickest way possible, sometimes skipping on accuracy just to get rid of him. They soon learned this didn't work: one of the odd things about the new Mark was that if there was anything he didn't understand – *anything* he didn't understand – he'd ask about it and expect an answer. He didn't notice when people were uncomfortable around him because he'd never seen what a comfortable person looked like.

Soon I forgot all about my own work and spent the lesson watching Mark cutting through the worksheets. He wasn't doing it competitively like some of the brainier kids, and he wasn't showing off or anything. He'd look at the sheets and then just do them.

'Hey, you're really good at that stuff!' I said as we got out of the lesson.

Mark accepted this with a nod.

'It's weird,' I said as we went to lunch. 'Mark was useless when it came to maths.'

'Bollocks,' Mark said. 'I've always kicked ass at maths. Just look at my reports.'

It took me a moment to answer; I needed a second to get over Mark's newfound attitude problem. Sure, the words were fine (well, okay, 'kicked ass'?), but instead of sounding aggressive they came out as if he was reading them politely from a phrasebook.

'I used to give you all the answers,' I told him.

'Oh.'

That was all he said. He sounded like I'd just played a cruel trick on him – not angry, just disappointed and humiliated. It was like I'd not only told him Father Christmas didn't exist, but that his colour scheme was a way of selling Coca-Cola.

'I mean, you did some of it yourself,' I added, 'and it wasn't like you *couldn't* do them; it's just, well, you were a lazy fucker.'

'Okay,' Mark said, looking directly at me. 'Listen, I've got to go down to the PE block to sign up for the football team. Want to meet at the art block afterwards?'

'Sure,' I said. 'Hey, Mark?' I added as he turned away.

He stopped.

'You're okay? I mean, you're not pissed off about the maths, are you?'

There was only a second's hesitation before he smiled and said, 'Nah, I'm fine. See you at the art block.' With that he left.

I was a little shocked. I still have no idea what went on with that Kwik-Learn thing, but I was pretty sure that the three days I'd known the clone were his first three days of real human interaction, and he was already learning how to lie.

Then another thing hit me: Mark and football. I thought about trying to catch up with him to explain, but then I remembered what happened with the maths. I didn't want to do that again, and besides, this Mark might be pretty good at football. Hell, he might even enjoy it.

Instead of chasing after him I wandered down to the dinner hall and got a veggie burger and chips. They were out of chicken burgers and the beef burgers looked as if they were meant to sole plimsolls.

At a table near the back of the hall I spotted Kirsty sitting on her own. She had a habit of doing that. After school and at weekends she had church groups and Young Christian weekends, but in school if you had the nerve to actually believe in anything you might as well turn up in a Starfleet uniform.

Okay, I'm sounding a little over-sympathetic here. I didn't necessarily think her beliefs were right, or that she was a very nice person, as I've already said, but even people you can't stand are people. Of course, at the time I wasn't even feeling that generous.

I walked over and sat opposite her.

'Hey! What was with you blanking Mark earlier?' I asked – well, less asked than accused.

She carried on eating as if I wasn't there.

'Oi! Pay attention when people are talking to you!'

She looked up and pulled her martyr face. 'If you want to play along with that charade it's your business. Personally, I'd rather stay out of its way.'

'You what?'

'If I was to accept that thing as Mark Self, it would be disrespectful to the real Mark.'

'What would he care?' I asked. 'According to you he's in heaven . . . probably.'

'But he's looking down on us,' Kirsty said.

'Yes, but what about the other Mark? The one that's alive?' I asked. 'Hell, you believe small clusters of cells have rights, so is it that hard to treat him like a person?'

'I can treat him as a person in his own right,' Kirsty said. 'Not as a friend who I know is dead.'

I was really pissed off with her now. Mark had *never* thought of Kirsty as a friend. What right did she have to get all high and mighty over respecting his memory? I was certain that was why I was pissed off with her; it had absolutely nothing to do with the niggling feeling she was right.

'Really, I don't see why you don't try to help him,' Kirsty said. 'I mean, why can't you support him in trying to accept he's a new and unique person?'

I just stared at her and fumed.

'He doesn't want to be a new and unique person,' I said. 'He wants to be Mark. It's the idea that he's Mark that keeps him going. I'm not taking that away from him.'

'But it's all a lie.'

'Yes, well you'd know all about that, wouldn't you?' I said, getting up to leave.

Kirsty ignored that and asked, 'Are you sure it's the clone who doesn't want him to be a new person?'

I glared at her. 'Bollocks,' I said, before turning round and storming out. I like to think that meant I'd won the argument.

I found Mark sat on the wall behind the art block. He was watching a sparrow hop around on the grass opposite. At least I thought he was at first. As I came closer I noticed that he wasn't actually looking at the sparrow, which was pretty weird for the clone. Mark's clone had never seen anything that he hadn't really *looked* at. Now his eyes were on the bird, but his mind seemed to be somewhere else.

'How'd footy practice go?' I asked, feeling I already knew the answer.

'I need a lot of practice,' Mark said, 'but I'm going to get better.'

He'd obviously been terrible. This bewildered him. Mark had always loved football, and although he'd never been able to actually play, he was sure that if he had been able to get out of his chair he'd have been a regular David Beckham. Well, that's my best guess at what was going on in the clone's head.

'Mark had a lot of other interests apart from football, you know,' I said as I sat down next to him.

'I know, I *am* Mark,' the clone said.

I reminded myself that he didn't want to be a new and unique person.

'Then you'll remember all your other interests,' I said, 'like . . . um . . . computer games, and films and other stuff.'

I realized that if Mark had any real interests I'd never learned about them. We played video games when I went round his house and sometimes got DVDs out when I stayed over. There was never anything he'd been truly passionate about. Or if there was, he simply hadn't let me in on it. That worried me. I'd always felt that I knew Mark better than anyone, better than his parents and sister, definitely better than would-be sympathizers like Kirsty. The idea that there was a part of Mark that he'd managed to keep from everyone, a bit of him that had just slipped out of existence in that hospital room, added a sudden punch to my feeling of loss.

Lauren and Kate were playing curby. Curby was like piggy in the middle, except that instead of a piggy, they had the road outside Kate's house. On the other side of the road was the Green, a threadbare grassy space where kids were supposed to play ball games – but they didn't because of all the dog poo.

Lauren and Kate stood either side of the road, tossing a ball between them. It was four o'clock. The school run had finished but people hadn't started coming home from work yet, so the girls largely had the road to themselves.

'Did you watch *Invasion of the Body Snatchers*?' Kate asked.

'It was lame,' Lauren said. 'You didn't tell me it was black and white.'

'It's not!' Kate shouted. 'I saw it round my brother's flat. It's in colour, and there's a bit where you see a guy's head split in two!'

'Liar,' Lauren said. 'I bet you didn't even watch it. I bet you were too scared!'

Kate was so angry she missed the ball, and the conversation had to pause while she ran on to the Green to fetch it.

'It's not even scary,' she said when she got back. 'Even if you became a pod person it wouldn't matter. I mean, you'd still look the same, you'd still have all the same memories, so how'd you know?'

Lauren wasn't going to admit that that made it worse. 'Throw the ball then!' she shouted.

'I'll bring the DVD into school next week,' Kate said once the ball was going again. 'That'll prove it!'

'I thought you were going to Disney World next week?'

'Nah. Disney World's for babies. My mum and Trevor are going there next week, but I get to stay at my brother's place. He's got digital TV, and an Xbox, and he lets me stay up as long as I like!'

Kate's brother was twenty-two, which seemed to Lauren impossibly old for a brother.

They continued passing the ball, considering the utopia of Kate's brother's flat.

'How's *your* brother?' Kate asked.

Lauren pretended not to hear.

'Because Daniel Spencer said that his brother is in your brother's class, and he says since your brother came back to school he's been a real spastic.'

'Daniel Spencer's a spastic,' Lauren said, and threw the ball too hard.

The ball pounded into Kate's hands and she jerked away.

'Ow!' she cried. 'You bent my finger back. Stupid!'

The ball rolled into the road.

'You better pick that up,' Kate said.

There was a rumbling in the distance.

'You pick it up, it's your stupid ball,' Lauren said, pouting.

'Don't sulk. Just 'cause your brother's a spastic,' Kate said.

Lauren looked daggers across the road. A red Peugeot had turned the corner and was slowly coming down the road.

'My mum told me what they did to your brother,' Kate said. 'She says people go to hell for doing things like that.'

The rumbling of the Peugeot's engine was getting louder, but to Lauren it didn't seem to come from down the road. It seemed to come from inside. From her head and her chest and her fists, which were suddenly clenched.

'She says that's why your brother's such a spastic,' Kate continued. 'It's because he's not got a soul like real people. Because only God can give people souls.'

Lauren didn't want to answer back. She didn't want to think. So she lowered her head and charged into the road, grabbing the ball and hurling it as far as she could.

There was a screech of brakes and the blare of a car horn. Lauren felt amazingly light, as if she was floating behind herself, running to catch up. Then she was on the other side of the road and the driver was getting out of the red Peugeot and shouting things that Lauren couldn't hear.

Kate and Lauren looked at each other, checked the driver of the car wasn't a teacher or neighbour, then swore at him and ran away laughing.

If the whole world was turned upside down, so that the sky was miles below us and the ground was above our heads, and we had to get from one house to another using tight-ropes and monkey bars, things would seem strange for maybe two or three days, possibly even a week. After that we'd settle back into the routine again and shimmy our way to school and work along the telephone lines, occasionally getting caught in traffic jams when too many people were trying to use the same line, or maybe complaining there weren't enough tightropes, or too many that spoiled the view.

Basically, no matter what disaster is thrown at us, we love normality so much we'll recreate it in no time. I talked to my granddad about the war once. He was ten or eleven at the time, and he went on for hours about gas masks and bomb shelters and evacuation. It all sounded really boring. He was living in terror of being blown to pieces every night by German planes, but all he seemed to want to talk about was some teacher who had a squint and that he had to wear short trousers all the time.

I didn't really understand that until a couple of weeks after I met Mark's clone. The fact was I couldn't worry over the clone all the time, any more than I could stay grief-stricken for Mark. I had homework to do, dishes to wash, TV programmes to watch, itches to scratch.

I soon fell into a routine with him. I'd meet him at his house; he'd greet me at the door with his latest attempt at sarcasm or casual insult. He'd get the words right, but he just couldn't get the feeling behind it. Sarcasm sounded like a foreign language when he used it.

We'd walk to school and Mark would ask me about some quirk of human nature that confused him. He could surprise me sometimes. He didn't understand why his sister always wanted the biggest portion of dessert, but in biology he was the only boy in the class who could say 'vagina' without giggling. The rest of the class loved this, naturally. At break several people cornered him and asked him to say it over and over. He did so, being the helpful person that he was, and watched in confusion as they fell about in hysterics. Mark kept repeating it when they asked until I suggested that perhaps it wasn't a good idea to say words like that on demand.

'Why? It's just a word,' Mark said.

'Well, yeahhh,' I said, dragging the 'yeah' out as far as possible, 'but you see, people find words to do with sex funny. So when people ask you to say them like that, they're sort of taking the piss.'

'Why are words to do with sex funny?' Mark asked.

I had to change the subject at this point because I knew that Mark was miles ahead of me. In fact I secretly suspected that Mark's willingness to perform for the other kids was down to more than mere helpfulness. Maybe I'd got it wrong about who was taking the piss out of who.

When he first came back, we had to run the gauntlet of the playground every day, but that wasn't so bad any more. People had just got used to us. After the first couple of weeks of taking the real Mark to school I'd practically forgotten about his wheelchair. Now I was beginning to forget about his clone-ness.

Football practice was a living hell for Mark. He went every Tuesday lunchtime without fail, and at registration I'd find him sitting alone in the classroom looking bewildered and upset. It wasn't surprising really. I'd seen him play in PE and he was truly awful. I've never been too good at sports myself, but Mark took bad playing to a whole new level. He would run after the ball, tripping over himself and booting himself in the arse, and on catching up with it he'd take a flying kick that sent the ball off at right angles.

It would have been funny if it wasn't so tragic. He'd go flailing around the pitch before attempting to score a goal into his own net, only to see it fly a mile wide. Then he'd do it all over again with as much determination and enthusiasm as before.

When I asked him about it afterwards he'd look a little doubtful and say he could do with improving and needed more practice, but was getting better and at least he was enjoying himself. The lies were as obvious as an extendable wooden nose. It wasn't that he was a particularly bad liar: lying was a skill he'd picked up far more quickly than his fumbling attempts at sarcasm. But while most of us sprinkle our daily lives with a liberal seasoning of white lies and delusions, Mark was helplessly honest as long as you didn't approach the issue of who he was.

Whenever I brought that up, I'd come up against a wall of minor lies ('I'm going to get better') and the sheer immovable faith that he *was* Mark Self, the same person I'd known since I started high school. You couldn't argue with it – you couldn't even try to ignore it. As time went on he clung to this idea more and more. I'd repeat some story about me and Mark and the clone would say, 'Oh? I'd forgotten we did that.'

More worryingly, I was finding it hard to draw the line between where one Mark ended and the other began. Like the time in the video store. We were combing the shelves for something with big explosions, lots of gore and questionable morals.

'How about this one?' Mark asked, pulling out a Vin Diesel movie.

'Tut tut,' I teased. 'Your mummy wouldn't want you watching something so violent.'

'I don't see why,' Mark said, totally missing the sarcasm. 'It's not like the people really die in it, they just fall over or get chopped in half or blown up in funny ways. That's not like *proper* dying.'

'Anyway,' I said, looking at the box again, 'didn't we see that one ages ago?'

'Did we?' Mark asked, looking confused.

'Yeah, when I stayed over for your birthday . . .'

Mark hadn't had a birthday. At least, his clone hadn't.

Lauren found life at home wasn't getting better exactly, but she felt she was getting used to it. Her mum had lied when she said they'd treat the clone just like the old Mark. Her parents never missed an opportunity to say how proud they were of him, or how much they loved him no matter what.

It was most obvious with her mum. When they sat down on the settee she'd put her arm around Mark and give him a cuddle. Mark would sit there passively, staring at the TV. Lauren hated her mum trying to cuddle her like a teddy bear, and if she'd tried it on her she would have beaten her off with cries of 'Awww, Muuum!' But sometimes Lauren wished her mum would at least try.

Maybe she was imagining it, but Lauren also got the feeling that her mum was disappointed when the clone didn't fight her off as well.

Her dad wasn't quite so obvious about it, but he was doing the same thing. He'd call the clone things like 'Good man!' and 'My boy!' all the time, which had sent Lauren into fits of giggles the first time she heard it. He'd never spoken to Mark like that when he was alive, so Lauren had no idea why he'd started now. She asked him once and her dad went red and shouted at her for being cheeky.

Then there was the football. Whenever it was on, the clone and Lauren's dad took over the living room. They used to do this when Mark was alive as well. Her dad would give Mark a beer, which he'd drink and then pull a disgusted face at, and they'd just sit there hurling abuse at the TV.

While this was going on, Lauren and her mum would go up to her mum's room and sprawl out on the bed with a box of chocolates and a couple of books. The chocolates were too sweet and had this sickly gooey stuff in the middle, and the books her mum read were really boring. They were all about women who wanted to have an affair with men who were richer or poorer than they were, and how everybody else didn't like it, and they were always set really far in the past, like the Middle Ages or the sixties. Lauren would much rather read some Jacqueline Wilson or a Point Horror.

But despite the sickly chocolates and her mum's boring books, Lauren had always liked those afternoons. Okay, so when the boys started shouting downstairs she would really have liked to be down there with them, but it wasn't too bad. It was like a secret girls' club or something.

Of course, the clone had managed to spoil even that. Lauren didn't know why it had been spoilt – she just knew it wasn't quite right. Like that time Mark had secretly put vinegar on her cornflakes.

For a start there was all that 'Good man!' stuff, and the

clone didn't react the same way to beer that Mark had. Instead of pulling a disgusted face, he'd take swigs of it, and then do one of his annoying little confused frowns. The shouting from downstairs didn't sound right either; she'd hear her dad leaping into the air and cheering about a second before the clone did, and then the clone would be trying too hard.

After the clone arrived, Lauren had looked forward to being stuck in Mum's room with the chocolates and the books again. Once she had Mum on her own, the clone wouldn't be able to push his stupid face in and ruin it all. Then she saw the books her mum was reading. Gone were *Love on a June Railway Track* and *The Candles of the Winter Dove*. Instead, there were lots of books with titles like *Key to Life* and *Cycle of the Soul*. They were all written by people with 'Prof' or 'Dr' or sometimes 'Rev' in front of their names.

Sometimes her mum would talk about what she was reading, things like hypnotism revealing past lives and genetic memory telling salmon where to breed. Soon Lauren took to reading her Point Horror in her bedroom with a packet of crisps and a Penguin from the cupboard downstairs. The sickly chocolates didn't taste right any more; it was like someone had put vinegar on them.

Mark bit his lip as his mum drew the blood from his arm. He focused on the pattern of the wallpaper and the sound of the traffic outside, focused on not focusing on the nauseating feeling of suction going on inside his arm. He didn't look back until his mum had drawn the blood, squirted it into a small plastic tube and bunged the cap into the top of it. On the table beside his mum was an array of samples: the swab that had been jabbed into Mark's cheek and sealed up in a ziplock bag, another bag containing a lock of Mark's hair, and now a plastic tube of black-red liquid.

'There, that wasn't so bad now, was it?' his mum said.

Mark shrugged. He'd had so many tests done on him over the years he'd stopped feeling anything about them. When he was little he would have screamed and fought and even kicked, back in the days when he could kick, to try and keep the evil nurses away with their needles and swabs and God knew what else. Now he accepted it as just another of life's inconveniences. They were always testing him for something, always trying some new, experimental treatment or other. These samples were just the latest of hundreds of tiny bits of Mark that had been to hospitals, clinics and labs all over the world.

Mark hadn't told his parents that he'd already given up, that when push came to shove he was ready to die. His mum wouldn't have been able to cope. His dad would have been okay, his dad always was, but even then Mark didn't relish the idea of actually saying, 'When the time comes, I don't really mind.'

His mum picked up the samples and placed them into a small plastic box filled with spongy padding. The word 'Proteus' was embossed in black, high-tech lettering across the lid.

'Now I'll just go and deliver these to the clinic. Are you all right being left on your own for a couple of hours?'

'It might just kill me,' Mark said darkly, then saw the pained expression on his mum's face. 'I'm kidding,' he said. 'I'll be fine, Mum.'

'You sure?' his mum asked.

'Yes, now get out of here!' Mark sighed.

His mum gave him a peck on the forehead, then left, cradling the box of samples in her arms.

Imitation

Imitation

I like Phil, but he can be very strange sometimes. Like, whenever we talk about things that happened a long time ago he stops talking, and all I can get out of him is a lot of grunts and mumbles. Then there's the way he looks at me sometimes. Most of the time, when we're doing things like picking a DVD or talking about homework, he talks as if I'm not really here. He glances at me and then looks at where he's walking, or what other people are doing, and keeps talking or listening the whole time. I've noticed lots of people do that. Two people will be walking along acting as if they are talking to each other, but when you listen to them it sounds as if they're both having conversations with themselves that happen to be going on at the same time.

But when I start talking about certain things, like football, or what we did last year, or things other people have said that confused me, he changes. He looks straight at me, like he's never seen me before.

He seems to know a lot more than me about things, although sometimes I think he gets confused. Like when we were planning my birthday. Every year for my birthday I go bowling with a couple of friends, before having a big family meal in the evening with lots of relatives. This year I wanted to go bowling with Phil, because of him being my best friend, and Kirsty, because she'd seemed upset last time I saw her and I wanted to cheer her up.

'I don't think that's a good idea,' Phil said.

He was looking everywhere except where I was sitting, but this time it seemed more deliberate than usual. He looked like the gerbil in our biology class when it's trying to find a way out of its cage.

'Why not?' I asked.

Phil took a deep breath and was quiet for a bit.

'She doesn't believe that you're really Mark,' he said.

I had to assume he was talking to me, because he was looking at his shoe, and although I didn't think Kirsty believed his shoe was really Mark either, I didn't think it needed to be told.

'Who else would I be?' I asked.

Phil took another deep breath, and started making noises like 'Um . . . well . . . err, you see . . .'

After a while he said, 'She thinks that because you're a clone, you're . . . well . . . a fake.'

'Oh,' I said.

I was a little confused, because I didn't understand how you could be a fake person, so I asked about that.

'Well, she thinks that you – that is, you the clone – are a different person from the Mark Self who went around in a wheelchair,' Phil explained, 'and that it's wrong for you to pretend that you're him.'

I nodded. Now I understood. She was confused because I'm not ill any more.

'Why does that mean I can't invite her out for my birthday?' I asked.

'You don't want to hang round with someone who thinks you're a fake, do you?' Phil said.

'Why not? *I* know who I am, and just because she's confused about it doesn't make her a bad person, does it? Not like Chaz.'

Phil was staring at me again.

'I suppose there's nothing wrong with asking,' Phil said eventually.

So I did.

At the end of school I went down to the lockers and met Kirsty as she was getting some stuff out of her locker.

She looked a bit shocked when I said hello, but not frightened like she had the first time.

'It's my birthday on Saturday, so I'm taking some friends out bowling. Want to come?'

Kirsty looked weird. I was beginning to think she was just a weird person generally.

'Umm . . . do you really want me to come?' she asked.

'Yes,' I said. 'If I didn't want you to come I wouldn't have asked you, would I?'

'No, I suppose you wouldn't,' Kirsty said. Then she seemed to change slightly, a bit like Phil when he's doing an impression of Chaz. First he'll be Phil, and then he'll pull a face and change the way he's standing, and he'll be Chaz. The same thing happened to Kirsty – except instead of Chaz she turned into Kirsty.

'I'd be glad to come,' she said.

I took her address down and said I'd pick her up around twelve. Well, my mum would be driving, but I'd be there too.

55

We stopped for Phil first.

'Umm . . . Mark?' he asked when he got into the car. 'Why have you brought your little sister along?'

I shrugged, which was something Phil had shown me how to do. 'She's a friend as well, isn't she?'

Phil looked like he was about to say something, then just sighed and sat back in his seat next to Lauren. Lauren didn't look very happy either, which I thought was strange because I couldn't think of a reason for her not to be happy – but Lauren often looks unhappy when she has no reason to be. I'd talked to Phil about this before and he explained that it was normal for little sisters to look like that.

Then we picked up Kirsty, and that was really funny because both the girls were acting like the gerbil in biology.

The bowling alley was amazing. Everything was clean and brightly coloured and there was music coming from all directions: mad chirpy music burst out of the penny arcades, bouncy, thumping music came from the dance machines, and all over the ceiling speakers played pop music over the top of that.

It looked impossible not to have a good time here.

'Can you believe this dump?' Phil laughed.

'Don't you like it?' I asked.

'I love it! It's so cheesy you could puke!' Phil said.

I couldn't see any cheese (there was a photo of a burger with something yellow on it, but it didn't look like the cheese we had at home).

'Where's the cheese?' I asked.

Lauren gasped. 'He doesn't mean actual cheese, moron,' she said. 'He means that it's all tacky and rubbish.'

'Don't worry,' Phil said. 'It's in a good way. It's like, it's okay to like really crap stuff, as long as you know it's crap.'

'But if you know it's crap . . .' I started, but at that moment the song on the ceiling speakers changed.

'Good God!' Phil said. 'They're still playing Blink-182!'

'I like Blink-182,' Kirsty said.

'You would,' Phil replied.

We decided to get some milkshakes before we went bowling.

We sat in the diner at a plastic table with two menus covered in sharp, transparent plastic that made a twanging noise when you flicked it. Once we'd all got our drinks Phil suggested that I open my present.

'Okay,' I said, and he passed me a parcel wrapped in paper with reindeer and snowflakes on.

'I never have any decent wrapping paper at home,' Phil said.

I unwrapped the present, but was careful not to tear the paper because it looked nice. It was a DVD called *The One Hundred Biggest Football F*** Ups!*

'It's to show you that you aren't the *worst* footballer who ever lived,' Phil said. 'Maybe only the hundred and first most terrible.'

It sounded insulting, but I'd learned that this was just a funny type of lie that friends told each other.

Kirsty passed me another parcel; this one was wrapped up in silvery holographic paper. I turned it over a couple of times before opening it, to see how the light reflected off it. It was pretty and I liked it. I looked up and saw Phil was looking at the present as well, but he didn't seem to like it. He was looking at it as if it was dangerous, as if Chaz would jump out when I opened it.

'What's wrong, Phil?' I asked.

Phil did the same funny impression Kirsty had done; he seemed to turn into Phil.

'Nothing,' he said. 'I was just wondering what Kirsty had bought you.'

'You looked a bit nervous. I was wondering why.'

Phil smiled, which was strange because he didn't look very happy. 'Just want to make sure she didn't buy you a packet of Polos.'

'Why would she buy me a packet of Polos?' I asked, before realizing. The parcel was too big, anyway. 'Oh! It's a joke!'

'Yes, Mark, it's a joke.' Phil smiled again, but this time he looked like he was actually happy.

I opened the present. It was a big box of chocolates, the ones that are smaller versions of the chocolate bars you get in newsagents.

'Thanks, Kirsty,' I said. 'I'll save these for later.'

For some reason Phil looked relieved.

'I haven't got you a present,' Lauren said.

She sounded . . . triumphant?

'Why not?' I asked.

'Why do you always have to ask questions about everything?' Lauren shouted. She stood up and stormed off into the toilets.

'Little sisters, eh?' I shrugged and tried to do a twisted smile like the ones I did in the home videos.

'I'll go and see what's up with her.' Kirsty smiled. 'I'm good with children.'

I thanked her, but when she was gone I noticed Phil was pulling the disgusted face he puts on whenever I eat cheese and onion crisps.

'What's with the face?' I asked.

'I just can't stand the way she's always interfering,' Phil said.

'I thought she was helping.'

'Yeah, to make herself look good.'

'What's wrong with trying to look good?'

Phil shifted uncomfortably in his seat. ' I just can't stand the way she always sucks up to him upstairs,' he said.

I looked up. 'The manager of the bowling alley?'

'God,' Phil said.

'Oh. What's wrong with trying to look good for God?'

Phil looked at me. 'Umm, nothing, I suppose. It's just I don't believe in him, so it seems a bit silly. Like she's being nice for the wrong reasons.'

'How can you be nice for the wrong reasons?' I asked. 'Isn't being nice always a good thing?'

'Mark?' Phil said.

'Yes?' I said, looking back at him.

'Shush now.'

Lauren stormed past the bowling aisles and into the Ladies. It was all very posh, with shiny red sinks surrounded by ceramic tiling, the wall above was just one long mirror. There was a woman touching up her mascara in the mirror, and Lauren felt embarrassed. She didn't need to go to the toilet; she just wanted to get away from the clone. She went into one of the cubicles and locked the door behind her. Like everything else, the cubicle door was dead posh, covered in a marble pattern of pastel shades of beige, mauve and grey. Only the nasty shiny toilet paper in the metal box on the wall spoilt the effect.

She sat on the toilet lid with her knees up by her chin so

her feet couldn't be seen under the door. Then she waited. She didn't know what she was waiting for exactly. Maybe for her mum to come in and say, 'It's okay now, the clone's gone away and your brother's come back, so we can all get back to normal.'

What she got was Kirsty coming in and saying, 'Lauren?'

Lauren saw her shadow moving along the floor tiles. Then Kirsty's eye appeared under the cubicle door.

'You can get arrested for that,' Lauren said, letting her feet drop.

'Can I come in?' Kirsty asked.

'No.'

'You look like you could use a chat.'

'How do you know? You can only see me from the knees down.'

'Well, you seemed pretty angry when you left us,' Kirsty said.

'None of your business.'

'Maybe not, but I'd still like to help.'

'Shove off.'

Kirsty went quiet, so all Lauren could hear was her own breathing and heartbeat and the distant rumble and clatter of the bowlers. She was aware of a choked feeling, not in her throat, but just under her ribcage. She sat down and looked up at the four walls that seemed a bit closer than they had a minute ago.

'You still there, Kirsty?' Lauren asked.

'I'm here for you.'

'Bog off.'

'Don't be like that,' Kirsty said kindly.

'Don't be like that,' Lauren mimicked.

Kirsty sighed. 'You're a lot like your brother, you know.'

'What would you know about it?' Lauren asked. 'All you ever did was patronize him and get all clingy.'

'He didn't know what to do when people were nice to him either.'

'There's nice and there's nauseating.'

Kirsty paused for a second, then said, 'That's a long word for a ten-year-old, isn't it?'

'Yeah, well. Some of us are born smart.'

Kirsty let out a short laugh.

'What's so funny?'

'You really do sound an awful lot like Mark,' Kirsty said. 'You're just as defensive. Just as obstinate when people are trying to help you. If I hadn't met Mark's clone I might even think it was genetic.'

'Maybe,' Lauren said, 'but I'm better looking.'

Kirsty let out one of her 'I'm-so-understanding' sighs. Lauren had heard about them through Mark. It made her want to puke.

'You really miss him, don't you?' Kirsty said.

Lauren opened the cubicle door. 'I'm going to go bowling,' she said. 'I feel like trying to knock stuff over.' Then she walked out, leaving Kirsty kneeling by the toilet door.

By the time Lauren came back me and Phil had hired the lane and changed our shoes. The new shoes were shiny and smooth, but kept pinching my feet in awkward places.

Lauren seemed to have forgotten she'd just run off after shouting at everyone. She strolled over, picked up the biggest ball she could find and said, 'So where do I throw this?'

'I think you're supposed to throw it at the pins over there,' Phil said.

It was his turn, not Lauren's, but Phil didn't seem to mind.

Lauren ran up to the bowling aisle and put all her might into swinging her arm forward and hurling the ball at the pins. It landed with a thud against the floorboards, then rolled sideways into the gutter.

'But that's good too,' Phil said.

Kirsty came back from the toilets and sat next to me. Lauren took another go, this time knocking over one of the pins, then came and sat on the other side of me.

'I'm glad we had that little talk,' Kirsty said. She reached past me to put her hand on Lauren's. 'You know, if there's ever anything you need . . .'

'Can I have your milkshake?' Lauren asked. 'I've finished mine.'

Kirsty smiled. It seemed to go up from her chin, reach her nose and then stop.

'Of course,' she said, and passed her drink to Lauren.

Lauren grinned and began to slurp noisily at it.

'Good,' Kirsty said. 'Now that's all over with we can get on with enjoying ourselves.'

As she spoke a trumpet fanfare announced that Phil had hit a strike.

I was puzzled. 'I thought we were already enjoying ourselves?'

Phil smiled. Lauren laughed so hard she sprayed Kirsty's milkshake all over the bowling balls.

'What's that? Six strikes? In ten goes? Wow, I must be slipping.'

'Sure, Mark.'

'And how many did you get? I forgot to count for some reason. I think it was the way your arms flail about just before you throw. It's mesmerizing.'

'Well, it's a little harder when you can't just aim that ramp thing and give the ball a push.'

'You can't keep blaming your disability your whole life, Phil. You've got to learn to grow beyond your gangly arms and total lack of hand-eye co-ordination. Really, you'll be a better person for it.'

'Sod off and die, Mark.'

Mark's mum's car stopped, and I plummeted back into the present day.

It was already dark when Mark dropped off Kirsty and me at the top of our street. The 'party' had been a lot easier after Lauren came back from the toilets. She was still uneasy around Mark, but she'd been able to enjoy herself. Maybe she was feeling better, but I think she just wanted to avoid Kirsty's sympathy.

To be honest, I'd been worried how Mark's birthday would turn out from the moment he told me Kirsty was invited. I'd sat in the car with bated breath, waiting for her to start preaching, and I can't describe how relieved I was when the parcel she'd brought turned out to be a box of chocolates.

However, barring Lauren's little outburst and Kirsty's enthusiastic do-gooding, the afternoon had gone without incident. We'd played a few games, chatted about school-work, me and Lauren had taken the piss out of Mark (Kirsty had leapt to Mark's defence at first, but Mark explained that it's the sort of thing that friends do) and a good time was had by all. The only time I was really worried again that afternoon was after the bowling, when the birthday cake was brought out.

The moment we started singing 'Happy Birthday' my eyes caught Kirsty's. Could she bring herself to sing 'Happy birthday, dear Mark'? On the second 'happy birthday' my eyes switched to Lauren, who hadn't even bothered with a present. What would *she* sing?

When we reached the third 'happy birthday' the 'dear' seemed to last for ever. And when at last we sang 'Mark' in unison, Lauren almost shouting the name, I sagged with relief.

We'd sat through the car journey in silence, and it looked like the walk home wouldn't be any different.

Kirsty walked alongside me without paying me any attention. Her back was straight and she looked directly ahead, although her head tilted back so that her nose was pointing over the rooftops. Her hair, which was red and curly, floated behind her in a way that would have looked nice on most girls. It made Kirsty look a bit like a teacher.

'So,' I said eventually, 'didn't feel like treating Mark like a "new and unique person"?' I don't know why I said it. Boredom? Curiosity? Sheer cruelty perhaps?

'What's that supposed to mean?' Kirsty asked.

'You treated him just as if he was Mark,' I said. 'Buying him a birthday prezzie when it was clearly not *his* birthday, signing his card "To Mark", singing him happy birthday ...'

Kirsty snorted, the most aggressive thing I'd ever seen her do.

'No need to be rude,' she said.

'No, I suppose not.'

We continued walking in silence. Kirsty might have been a good Christian, but she was nothing like Mark. This silence wasn't an absence of talking, it was breathing space to regroup for another attack.

'At least I didn't encourage him to *mimic* Mark,' she said.

'What's that supposed to mean?'

'I don't know what those scientists taught him about being Mark,' Kirsty said pompously, 'but I'm pretty sure sarcasm wasn't on the curriculum.'

'He picked that up himself, and not very well either.'

'Who did he pick it up from, Philip?'

'I don't know! Around.'

'Are you saying you've never helped him, never tried to explain it to him, never told him that the old Mark did things differently?'

Without realizing it, we'd both stopped in the middle of the pavement.

'Of course I have. He's a mate, I help him out.'

'Even when he's trying to be someone he's not?' Kirsty said in what she thought was a knowing tone of voice. 'Mark, the clone Mark, just isn't naturally bitter like the old Mark was. He's kinder, more innocent, more trusting . . .'

As she spoke something hot and red began to rise inside me until I couldn't hold it any longer.

'You two-faced *bitch*.' I shouted the last word; it was either that or slap her one. 'You knew fuck all about Mark! You were just "the interfering cow" to him and you *dare* to pretend you understood him? And then you insult him?

Well maybe he was bitter, but I'll tell you this for nothing, at least he was fucking honest about it!'

I started walking again, but barely got six feet before I had to turn round and yell 'Bitch' again.

It wasn't long before I'd lost her, and I was glad. There was nothing in the world except me, the dark orange of the night, the streetlights and the occasional shouted swear-word. I sat on a garden wall and put my head in my hands.

'Phil?' Kirsty said.

I looked up and she was standing in front of me.

'What are you doing here?' I asked. 'Isn't your house back that way?'

'I couldn't go home without apologizing first. I shouldn't have said that about Mark. I shouldn't even have compared the clone with Mark.'

I shrugged. 'It's impossible not to, really.' I was feeling generous. If she was big enough to apologize, so was I . . .

'But I stand by everything I said before that. You're not making him any happier by teaching him all the things that made Mark miserable.'

I got up to leave.

'Phil! Wait.'

'Why? So you can explain exactly how I'm corrupting your sweet innocent little clone? So I can hear you bad-mouth my best mate? Sorry, I've got better things to do.'

'Okay, you're right,' Kirsty said.

She didn't say it in an apologetic way. She said it in the kind of way that meant, 'Look how big I'm being, admitting I'm in the wrong when I'm not really.'

Then she added, 'Just ask yourself this. Have you felt easier around him recently?'

'Sure I have. I've got to know him better.'

Kirsty tilted her head in a way that was supposed to

make her look concerned. 'Have you, Phil? Have you really?' she said in her best mystic voice.

Then she turned and walked off.

'Bollocks!' I shouted after her.

Somehow I didn't feel I'd won that round.

'I wasn't singing happy birthday to *you*, you know.'

Lauren hadn't said a word to me all the way home, until she came into the bathroom, where I was getting ready for dinner that evening. She'd come to tell me that she wasn't singing 'Happy Birthday to You'.

'Oh?'

I'd discovered 'Oh?' was a pretty useful noise. It often seemed like people were talking to me but didn't want me to actually say anything, but because it was a conversation I had to say something at some point, if only to give the other person time to breathe. 'Oh?' was perfect. It meant I was just putting the full stops in other people's sentences.

I turned back to the bathroom mirror and combed my hair.

Lauren stood in the doorway, arms crossed, brow furrowed, one foot tapping. 'Oh' hadn't worked. I put my comb down.

'Why weren't you singing "Happy Birthday to You"? I thought I heard you singing it.'

She groaned. 'You're so stupid!' she said. 'I was singing "Happy Birthday to You", I just wasn't singing "Happy Birthday to You" to *you*.'

It took me a moment to understand this sentence.

'Who were you singing it to then?' I asked.

'I was singing it to my brother. It's his birthday.'

'You have another brother?'

'Duh! Mark, the *real* Mark.'

'That's me,' I said.

She came in and stood next to me, on tiptoe so she could see into the mirror. I'd been there for a long time, combing my hair. I'd tried combing it back and to the side and forward, doing it neatly, or messing it up, but it still didn't look right.

'You never told me,' she said. 'What *did* you think of our bedroom in Devon?'

I'd been thinking about this since she first asked me, trying to remember. I remembered that we'd been there from the twenty-eighth of June to the fourteenth of July. I remembered that we'd gone to the beach a few times, and that on a couple of days we'd been able to sunbathe but it had rained the rest of the time. I remembered some of the photos we'd taken, Dad buried up to his neck in sand, Mum hiding from the camera, nine-year-old Lauren building a sandcastle. Yet I couldn't remember how I *felt* about any of it.

'You've no idea, have you?' Lauren said.

'I . . . liked it?'

Lauren shook her head. 'It was horrible. We only had a tiny bunk bed between us, and Mark was always complaining because I kept dropping Rabbit on his head. Once he threatened to feed Rabbit to the seagulls if I dropped him again, so I screamed and Mum and Dad came and we both got grounded. We were stuck in the caravan for three days after that and argued the whole time.'

She sounded the way Phil had done when he was talking about how I'd been before. It was silly, but she sounded like she *wanted* to argue all the time. I knew we used to argue a lot on holiday, but I'd always thought of it as a bad thing. One of the things people don't make home movies about. Now I thought about it I got the feeling that maybe people still wanted to remember the bad things, but somehow even the bad things were better in the old days.

'I remember we had a lot of arguments,' I said.

'You weren't there.'

She had a small smile on her face when she was talking about the arguments in the caravan, so small I didn't notice it until it was gone.

I wanted to say something then. I didn't know what it was I wanted to say, I just knew I wanted to bring that smile back, to make everything okay.

'Lauren,' I began.

'Mark! Lauren! The others will be here soon. Come and help set the table,' Mum shouted from the kitchen.

Lauren turned away from the mirror and looked me up and down. 'You don't even look like him,' she said and went downstairs.

The birthday meal looked nice. Mum had got pizza and crisps and potato salad and sausages on sticks and some barbecued chicken and hamburgers and chips, all laid out on paper plates with 'Happy Birthday' printed around the edge in primary colours. Once we'd set the table she poured us each a glass of soft drink, cool and inviting with little sparks of fizz leaping around the surface like a flea circus.

I reached for my drink.

'Not yet, Mark,' Mum said. 'We have to wait for the guests to arrive.'

So I sat and waited.

After a while the flea circus settled, and the little bubbles that were rushing up from the bottom of the glass stopped. The paper plates grew damp grey shadows where the food was, the chips sagged and the pizza topping looked like a twelve-inch-wide scab.

Mum's mouth became thinner and her face changed colour. Dad put his hand out towards her once and she jerked away.

Lauren stood up.

'Where are you going?' Mum asked. It sounded more like a threat than a question.

'*EastEnders* is on. I'm going to watch it in my room.'

'Sit down, young lady. The guests will be arriving any minute. You will not go swanning off to watch some trashy soap.'

'I thought you liked *EastEnders*?' I asked.

Mum looked a little shocked, like she always does when I ask a question.

'Yes, Mark dear, but there are more important things than television.'

'This is stupid!' Lauren said, stamping her feet. 'We've been sat here for ever!'

Mum opened her mouth to reply, but was interrupted by the doorbell.

'I wonder who this could be?' Mum said. Her face was smiling but her voice was shaking.

Aunty Jane was at the door. She's my mum's sister. I like Aunty Jane – she used to bring me and my sister presents whenever she visited and was always laughing and joking around when I was little. She has dark brown curly hair and her skin's a little bit wrinkly but not wrinkly enough to make her look old. I'd seen lots of photos of her and she was always smiling.

When she came into the dining room her hair looked dead, which was silly because hair isn't alive in the first place. She didn't have many more wrinkles than in the photographs, but somehow they were working twice as hard to make her look old.

'Hello, Lauren,' she said as she came in. Then she looked at me, stared for a long time and said, 'Hello, Mark?'

'Hi, Aunty Jane!' Lauren said, running over to hug her.

I went and hugged her too, but she seemed to stiffen when I did.

'Where's Gerald?' Mum asked.

She meant Uncle Gerald, Aunty Jane's husband. The question sounded like it was made of metal.

'He's working late,' Jane said quietly.

'Ah. Do you know if Mum's coming?'

'She's feeling ill. She sends her apologies,' Jane said.

'Of course she does,' Mum said, as if sending apologies was something bad, but something she'd expected, like Lauren leaving her room a tip.

Everyone stood in silence for a moment, Mum staring at Jane, Jane staring at her feet and Dad standing by the table, looking as if he wanted to leave.

'Shall we sit down to dinner?' Mum asked. 'I'm afraid it's all gone a bit cold.'

We served ourselves helpings of everything, including the stuff we didn't like. I found it didn't matter anyway – the food had a funny, cardboardy taste, apart from the chicken, which was like slimy rubber. The Coke was luke-warm and tasted like sweetened water.

'How are you doing in school, Mark?' Jane asked without looking at me.

'I'm doing okay. I'm doing well in maths, but English is quite hard and I'm getting better at football.'

'You're still football mad then?' Jane said, smiling weakly.

'Oh yes, he's crazy about it, aren't you, Mark?' my mum said, and she laughed, but it sounded dry and scratchy.

I nodded, and chewed on a slice of pizza.

The whole evening went that way. It was a birthday party and people were supposed to be happy, so everybody smiled and chatted and said things that sounded like jokes and made people laugh, but weren't actually funny. I did it too, and I didn't know why. Mum was cross because Aunty Jane was the only person who came to my party, and Dad was worried because of Mum, and Lauren was grumpy because of *EastEnders*, and Jane was looking tired and sad and although it was my birthday nobody had actually asked me whether I was enjoying it or not. So who were we trying to convince?

I regretted blowing my top at Kirsty. Sort of. She had no right to say the things she did, but by the time I was in bed I realized how thickly I'd been laying it on. Worse still, part of me knew she had a point.

I'm not sure how much of it was down to the clone's imitation getting better, or more worryingly, how much was down to my memories of Mark beginning to fade, but it was getting harder to remember that Mark Self and Mark Self's clone were different people. When I was reminded, it was like seeing Father Christmas's beard pulled off – you could put the beard back again and try to forget it happened, but you'd be that little bit more reluctant to sit on his lap . . .

Take the time I was telling him about Sadie Goodman. Sadie really *enjoyed* talking about mobile phone covers, *Big Brother* and *Pop Idol*. If you asked her about hobbies she'd tell you they were 'Shopping and doing stuff.' She was also blond, had a below-average number of zits for our year and had been blessed (or cursed) with bigger tits than any non-fat girl in the school.

Whenever I spoke to her I talked too much and laughed too loud, but I wanted to speak to her all the time. I believed with all my heart that *this* was true love. The words of everything from Shakespeare's sonnets to Britney Spears songs all seemed to have been written specifically with me in mind.

Romeo and Juliet, Leonardo diCaprio and Kate Winslet, Mickey and Minnie Mouse and Phil and Sadie. You know, the romances that are just meant to be.

The week before Mark's birthday I was staying over at the clone's house and we were discussing exactly which *Buffy the Vampire Slayer* character was fittest. To be honest I wasn't interested in which *Buffy* character was fittest – I watched for the story and the cool one-liners – but I was thirteen now, and breasts were supposed to take priority. As for Mark, the clone, he was acting the sexist prat almost as well as I was – eagerly discussing Alyson Hannigan's tits in a way that was eerily similar to the old Mark – and I didn't notice.

As the conversation drew to a close I brought up Sadie. I expected him to take the piss, as Mark would have done, viciously and with good cause. He would have brought out his air violin. He would have sniffed, wiped a tear from his eye and said, with great feeling, 'My little boy's finally growing up' or 'But Phil, I thought *I* was your true love!'

I'd have responded with my middle finger, or two of them, and told him to fuck himself with a pineapple. Then we could have started talking about monster trucks, or whether you'd explode if you farted and sneezed at the same time.

'Why don't you ask her out?' the clone said.

'I can't do that!' I said, as if he'd suggested I serenade her wearing nothing but a fig leaf and chocolate body paint.

'Why not?'

'Because she might say no!'

'So? You'd be no worse off than you are now, would you?'

I thought about the serenading, the fig leaf and the body paint.

'You don't know that!'

'Isn't the whole point in asking somebody out to find out if they'll go out with you?' Mark asked.

'No!' I said with certainty. 'No, it definitely isn't. You only ever actually ask somebody out if you actually definitely know they'll actually definitely go out with you. Otherwise it would just be stupid.'

'How do you know if they'll go out with you?'

'Well, there are signs, you know? Things to look out for.'

'Like what?'

'You know! Things. Stuff, like fluttering eyelashes and things . . .'

'So if they flutter their eyelashes at you they'll go out with you?'

'Maybe,' I said, although I'd never seen a girl flutter her eyelashes outside Disney cartoons, 'but they could be taking the piss. A lot of girls pretend that they're interested in you just to watch you squirm.'

'How do you tell the difference between girls taking the piss and girls wanting to go out with you?' Mark asked. 'Wouldn't it be easier to just ask them?'

I had no idea. All I really knew about asking girls out was that it was their playing field, their ball, they made the rules and they weren't going to tell us what the rules were.

'You know, when we used to talk about stuff like this all Mark did was rip the piss, make a joke of it and then we didn't have to worry about it any more. We didn't have big in-depth discussions about it.'

'Oh,' Mark said.

A few days later Sadie actually fluttered her eyelashes at me. I did what any sensible guy would do and ran off to find Mark.

'Sadie fluttered her eyelashes at me!' I told him between gasps of breath – I'd been running pretty fast to find him.

'Probably had something in her eye,' Mark said.

He hit the tone just right, like a wasp sting on the nose.

I lay in bed thinking about this the night of Mark's birthday. The real Mark, no, not the real Mark, the real *clone* of Mark, would have asked lots of questions, would have wanted to know exactly what it meant. The day the clone just brushed me off I felt I'd lost something, which was stupid. How could I be losing something if he was becoming *more* like the person I knew?

I didn't get much sleep that night. I lay in bed with nothing to do but remember my argument with Kirsty, my chats with the clone, my memories of Mark. I thought about apologizing to Kirsty, but that would just give her another chance to have a go at me. I'd apologized to her in my head. I did feel sorry for the things I'd said, but I'd be damned if I'd let her know that.

When I saw Kirsty in the corridor on Monday she just

nodded, said hello and kept walking, but I still kept thinking back to the argument and all the dangerous thoughts it had thrown up. Whenever the lessons got boring my mind would drift off to that orange-lit street, or to Mark, the old and the new, and I'd feel I was somehow betraying both of them.

Meanwhile, Mark decided to ask me how the brain works.

'Phil, how does the brain work?' he said.

'I don't know. Ask Mr Jones,' I said.

'I don't think a biology teacher can tell me what I want to know,' Mark said. 'Biology is all about the gooey sticky parts of the brain, and that's interesting, but not what I'm confused about.'

Realizing that asking this was like painting yourself with honey and rolling into a nest of flesh-eating ants, I said, 'What is it you're confused about?'

'You know how sometimes you think things even though you don't want to think about them, or you do things even when you know you shouldn't, or believe things even when you know they aren't true?' Mark asked.

'Uh huh.'

'Well, if it's your brain doing the thinking and the decision making and the believing, then who is it that doesn't want to think about things, or knows you shouldn't do things or that things aren't true?'

'A different part of the brain?' I suggested.

'But really you're made up of the things that you think and feel, right?' Mark said. 'So if you *are* your thoughts and feelings, why does it feel like thoughts and feelings are things that happen to you?'

I was amazed. I know I should have been used to it by then, but I was gobsmacked anyway. Mark was looking at me, and God help me, he actually expected an answer. The greatest minds in history had spent centuries studying the human condition and were still stumped, but here was Mark, standing in front of me, smiling, asking a question and expecting me to just *tell him*.

'I don't know!' I said. 'Why do you keep asking me stuff as if I'm Einstein or something? I don't know any more than you do! In fact, most people don't. The only difference is we just accept the fact that we can't know everything and get on with our lives.'

Mark looked at me with those wide, baby-like eyes, eyes that still looked at the world in amazement despite the sarcasm and the swearwords. He looked at me and said, 'Okay.'

I hated myself then. I didn't know why I'd said that. Maybe it was because when you feel things are getting bad you want to prove it by making things worse. But I knew one thing for certain – I understood what Mark meant when he talked about the mind being something that happens to you.

Mark didn't ask any more questions that day, not of me, not of the teachers (who were visibly relieved), not of anyone. That afternoon we walked back to Mark's house and he just moaned about the teachers being crap and Chaz being a moron, and sounded all the time almost exactly like my old friend. It felt shitty.

Then we got to his house and discovered that Mark's sister was dead.

After his mum left with the samples, Mark sat for a bit, content with his own thoughts. Then, when he was sure she wasn't going to burst back in, he wheeled himself over to the computer in the dining room.

When Phil was sleeping over, one of the games they played was 'Things to Do before You Die'. It was a simple game, and nobody ever mentioned that one of the contestants had less time than the other. All they did was lie awake in bed and compile a to-do list, categorizing the tasks by priority, likelihood or just how good the suggestion was.

The top of the list was always the same: Have Sex. Other favourites included egging Mr Jones, driving a limousine into a swimming pool, getting so drunk you puked and swimming with hammerhead sharks. (That one had started off as swimming with dolphins, but Mark had decided that was too sissy.)

They'd even managed to achieve a couple of the things on the list. Four cans of Stella had been enough to achieve goal number three, although after that everyone's parents had got angry and concerned and Phil hadn't been allowed over for a week. Now that Mark had the house to himself he had the perfect opportunity to achieve goal number twenty-eight.

Mark would never admit it to Phil, but he wasn't exactly sure why looking at a lesbian porn website was on the list. They'd been competing again, and somehow they'd got on to the topic of pornography. Then Phil had decided it should be lesbian pornography. Mark had suggested animal pornography, just to gross Phil out, but Phil had pointed out that animals were naked anyway, so what was the point?

Truth be told it didn't matter why looking at lesbian porn was on the list, it just was. Once a task was written it *became Mark's duty to do it if the opportunity arose. He powered the computer up, and cringed as the musical chords rang throughout the house to let him know he was using Windows XP. There was no one in, so Mark needn't have worried, but he still felt a twang of guilt as he logged on to the Internet and brought up Explorer.*

He clicked on the address bar and began to type. He'd intended to put in www.lesbianporn.com and just hope a good website came up, but he was getting a spell of the chills again and his fingers moved slowly. By the time he typed the third W, a full stop and the L, a list had appeared under the address bar.

At the top of the list was www.laz-r-us-services.com in small black lettering. Curious, Mark clicked on it. It took a few minutes for the website to load, and Mark nearly got bored and logged off. When the website finally came up, he almost wished he had.

Replica

Replica

When Phil and me got home my parents looked strange. Mum was on the settee, while Dad was pacing up and down near the dinner table. They looked like they couldn't see each other. In fact it seemed like they couldn't see anyone, as if they thought everybody else in the world had vanished.

I felt funny, like someone had stuffed something solid behind my ribcage. It didn't feel good. I don't know why I had that feeling: all that was different was that I couldn't hear Lauren playing her music upstairs, and Mum and Dad were acting weird. People act weird all the time – just when you think you know how they work they do something else that doesn't make sense – but this was different. It felt dangerous.

'Where's Lauren?' I asked.

I should have asked, 'Why are you two acting so weird?'

That question would have made sense, but suddenly I really needed to know where Lauren was. Mum and Dad stared at me as if they'd only just noticed I was there. I turned round to see where Phil was and realized he was still standing by the front door.

'There's been an accident,' Dad said.

'What sort of accident?'

A plane passed overhead. Somewhere, a long way away, somebody was playing tennis, or cricket or something. A dog barked. I could hear traffic, or perhaps a train in the distance.

Mum tried to tell me what had happened, but began crying. That scared me most of all. I don't know why, but I had this idea that mums weren't supposed to cry. They were supposed to be happy or tired or cross, they could smile or laugh or groan or shout or frown or wear party hats and sing, but they shouldn't cry.

And the word 'cry' isn't very good either. When you say 'cry' people think of just a few tears and some sniffing. When people write it down it's spelled 'boo-hoo' and that doesn't work at all. My mum sounded like a seal barking for fish, her face was all red and she was gasping for breath through the tears, and when she breathed through her nose there was a horrible snorting gurgling sound like someone blowing their nose backwards. She'd try and say something, but she couldn't sob, breathe and speak at the same time, so the words spluttered into nothing.

'Lauren was playing at Kate's after school,' my dad said. 'They were playing in the road, a car took the corner too quickly and hit Lauren. She was killed instantly.'

I realized he wasn't looking at me, but past me, at Phil.

'Jesus . . .' Phil whispered behind me.

I felt the bottom of my stomach, which had been filling up with lead, suddenly drop away to leave me free falling while standing still. I felt I needed to say something, but I didn't know what. I tried to follow Phil's lead and said, 'Fuck.'

It didn't feel right somehow.

'There's no need for bad language, Mark,' Mum said automatically.

'Leave him, Angela,' my dad answered.

For a second my mum seemed to notice that we existed, me and Dad. She stared at us, her eyes sore and red.

The video recorder made a kind of whining-humming sound when it was left on, and it seemed to be getting louder as we stood there. Soon I thought the windows might crack and cars would veer off the road into lampposts and dogs would go wild all because of that sound.

'I should go,' Phil said.

He was still standing by the door. His shoulder was trying to leave while his legs were rooted to the spot.

'You don't have to . . .' my dad said.

Phil seemed almost in physical pain. 'Yes I do,' he answered, and the door slammed behind him as he left.

I felt the floor drop slightly as the door slammed, like a lift when it starts going down. Phil seemed to have been a shield – as long as he was here it was as if we had to pretend everything was okay. It didn't matter that my sister had just died – when we had visitors my parents still wanted everything to be normal.

Once Phil had gone everything seemed to become more real. We sat in silence for a bit longer. Dad got up and went into the kitchen. Mum had forgotten we existed again, and was now staring at a patch of carpet. I wondered what she saw there.

I tried to work out what it meant now my sister was dead. I mean, I knew what it meant. I'd never see her again, never talk to her. It meant she'd never know what happened next in *EastEnders* or read the last Harry Potter books. I knew all this, but a world without my little sister in it just didn't work. She had to be here, to sulk and get told off and gasp as if everyone was stupid but her. That's what she was *for*.

I had hundreds of questions I wanted to ask. Where was Lauren's body now? Would Mum and Dad clone her so that she could come back and read the rest of the Harry

Potter books? Why did she have to die now, when things at home had seemed damp and miserable, so that the last thing she remembered was feeling cross? Why was life so unfair?

I didn't ask any of these questions. After all, Phil had explained that everybody had questions like that, and you didn't hear them going around asking about everything, did you?

So instead I went to my bedroom.

This time, when I fled the Selfs' house, there was no coming up for air, no relief. Instead the horrible dizzy feeling followed me up the road, dancing round me and making my insides squirm.

The clone had never had to deal with death before. Sure, he must have learned something about grieving just from listening to his mum, but as far as I knew he'd never had to deal with the fact that everybody died, and that sometimes this happened suddenly to people who didn't deserve it.

So Mark was going to be confused, and want things explaining to him, and it was going to be muggins here who'd be put up to the job. His mum would be no help – she'd be finding solace in her books, books about the psychic links between twins, or genetic theories on personality disorders. Books that said you didn't have to worry about this sort of thing, because people *don't really die.*

I was a little pissed off about that.

And what about me? How was I supposed to feel? I mean, how are you supposed to feel about the death of your best mate's sister? I'd never known her that well, and most of what I did know about her was what I heard through Mark. She was a bit of pest, but I liked her, I was used to having her around. There was this bizarre sense that I didn't have the right to be upset. I could only get my grief second-hand through Mark.

When I got home *The Simpsons* was starting in the living room. It seemed wrong.

'Hi, Phil,' my dad shouted from the kitchen.

I could hear pots bubbling, and he was wearing the apron with comedy tits on, so he must have been cooking. I went into the living room and sat in front of *The Simpsons*. It was one I'd seen.

How could people do that? Just get on with their lives while the world was falling apart just down the road? How could I do that? Why was I able to just come home and watch *The Simpsons* and eat my dad's pasta carbonara after what I'd just seen?

I let out a short laugh, but it wasn't at *The Simpsons*. Christ, I thought, I'm starting to sound like the clone.

The next day Mark came into school, as I had no doubt he would. I think he understood that his house was filled with a kind of insanity; even before Lauren died he'd used me as a way to escape from it. Sometimes it would be to ask me about the things they did that confused him, but I think mainly it was because he understood that his parents had created him with a certain picture in mind and every time he broke away from that picture he hurt them in a way that went right to the bone. I liked to think that when he was with me he didn't have to try so hard.

Today the insanity would be at its height and I guessed correctly that Mark would do his best to get out of it. This was the one correct guess I was going to make that day.

'Hiya, Butt-face,' Mark greeted me at the end of his road – he hadn't even bothered to wait for me.

'Hi, Mark,' I said. 'Is everything okay?'

I hadn't meant to sound cautious or concerned. I knew that wouldn't help and that the best thing I could do was act naturally, to try and make whipped cream out of lead.

'Yeah,' Mark said. 'I just had to get out of the house today. You get scared to breathe too loudly there at the moment.'

I was speechless. The clone had managed some pretty good approximations in the past, but when he spoke then he *was* Mark Self. Everything about him, his posture, facial expression, his voice, the look in his eyes, it was all exactly like the person who'd sat with me on the edge of the school disco, slurping Panda Pops.

'Mark?' was all I could answer.

He looked at me. I mean really looked at me. This wasn't looking as a way of seeing something – this was looking as a form of communication.

'Seriously, mate, are you all right? I mean, with your sister dying . . .'

'One less person fighting over the zapper,' Mark said with a shrug.

I was lost. I felt like slapping him, and felt guilty for it straight away. It wasn't as if it was my sister, and maybe this was his way of dealing with it. I didn't know what to do. Planet Phil was light years away and I had a feeling we weren't even in orbit round Planet Mark. I felt like I was with a violent sleepwalker. I'd heard that if you woke a sleepwalker they would die instantly, so you just had to walk alongside them, nudging them out of the way of fast-moving vehicles and bottomless pits, and just hope they woke up.

I was wrong again. I soon found out that this Mark was actually a hell of a lot easier to deal with. When people in the corridors called him a name or tried to trip him up, instead of asking why it had to happen he gave them a one-fingered salute and walked on, sometimes muttering 'Wankers' under his breath. In class when he got to a question he didn't understand he didn't ask me or the teacher for help, he just wrote down the best guess he could come up with and kept going.

I had a feeling that this was wrong – when your little sister died unexpectedly you didn't get *more* normal. What was worse was knowing that something was wrong and not being able to do anything about it. I knew that he must have been suffering somehow, but he showed no sign. If I'd brought the subject up he'd have made a flippant comment and got on with whatever he was doing.

When school finished I felt more relieved than I had in a long time to be getting away from him. I didn't know why the new, normal Mark was more disturbing than the weirdo I'd got to know over the last couple of months, but he was and I wanted out. It wasn't just that he was now inseparable from the old Mark, or that he was acting 'normally' when most people would be having a breakdown. I *think* it was because as long as I'd known the clone I'd known what he was thinking, not through any deep connection or intuition, but because if he was thinking something he said it. Now he had this mask on I was worried for the friend behind it. Worried for or scared of.

I was almost holding my breath as we approached the end of his road. Mark was talking about something dumb

Mr Jones had said in biology, doing a pretty spot-on impression while he was at it.

I turned to go down his road, when Mark said, 'I don't feel like going home yet.'

I froze. I hadn't known this was coming, but the second he said it I knew I should have.

'Want to come round mine?' I offered.

'Nah,' Mark said. 'Let's go somewhere else.'

'Where?' I asked.

Mark shrugged, and grinned the easy, crooked grin of a ghost I'd known. 'I don't know,' he said. 'Let's see where we end up.'

Earlier that day Kirsty wandered past the changing rooms. She didn't know why (*Yes you do*, a nasty voice at the bottom of her brain piped up): it was just lunchtime and she didn't have anywhere else to be. (*Funny how you had somewhere else to be on Monday,* the voice continued, *and you'll have somewhere else to be on Wednesday, won't you? But there's something about Tuesdays.*)

She was mildly surprised to hear the footballers coming back from practice. (*Yeah, because you had* no idea *that football practice was on Tuesdays, did you?*)

'Oh,' she thought to herself, 'I might go and check on Mark if he's around.'

(*Now there's an idea. Fancy that!*)

She turned back towards the boys' changing rooms, but the footballers were already inside. For no particular reason she decided to read the PE department's notice-board.

(*How convenient.*)

Kirsty leaned against the radiator opposite. Exactly what it was radiating she wasn't sure, but heat wasn't it.

The noticeboard held the cross-country leagues, relevant newspaper clippings and the school's one inter-school award (third place in a football tournament), along with posters telling children that javelins weren't toys and that running was dangerous without the appropriate warm-up. She read the clips avidly and then, when they were finished, decided to count the number of tiles on the ceiling.

(*It's not him, you know.*)

'I know!' the top part of her brain whispered back. Whispered, because if you didn't whisper, you'd realize you were paying attention to the bottom brain, which was just a nasty, bullying attention seeker.

(*Of course, but he still looks the same, doesn't he? Except taller of course. You never noticed how tall he was when he was stuck in that chair, did you?*)

'He's only a few months old,' the top brain said.

(*Yeah, but he doesn't* look *a few months old, does he?*)

'Yes, he does,' Top Brain said triumphantly. 'You just have to look into his eyes. Always wide open and gazing around. They *look* like baby's eyes . . .'

(*Yes, he needs someone to look after him, doesn't he?*)

'Shut up.'

(*Just like the* real *Mark needed someone to look after him, right? Except* that *Mark didn't want your help, did he? That Mark was mean and nasty, wasn't he? And now there's this new Mark, a* nice *Mark. Almost too good to be true, isn't it?*)

'Stop being stupid!' Kirsty hissed.

'Excuse me?' Mark asked.

'Sorry! Not you,' Kirsty stammered while Bottom Brain sniggered.

'Well, I don't see anyone else out here,' Mark said, looking at her like . . . like the real Mark had done.

'Hey! You're in there!' Chaz shouted as he came out of the changing rooms. 'Just tell her Jesus cured you!'

Mark gave him the finger without turning round.

'Are you all right?' Kirsty asked.

Mark had been trying almost from day one to be aggressive and nasty, but he'd never succeeded. Part of her (not Bottom Brain: Bottom Brain would scorn the idea as false hope) wondered if this was the clone, or the real Mark come back from the dead.

'Never better.' Mark grinned.

Kirsty shuddered.

'You don't look all right,' Kirsty said, trying to keep her voice calm and soothing. 'You look like something's bothering you. This isn't like you at all, Mark.'

(*That's a lie,* Bottom Brain said, seeming to side with Mark. *He's* exactly *like him.*)

'Would you like to talk about it?' Kirsty asked.

'Yes, I would,' Mark said sincerely, leaning against the radiator next to her. 'You see, this scrawny ginger nut who a couple of weeks ago couldn't even answer a hello without running off to puke is now trying to act like my best buddy so that she can feel like a saint, when I really need her help like a fish needs a caravan.'

(*He's back*! Bottom Brain chanted. *And he's right on form!*)

'Mark, you aren't like this,' Kirsty said.

(*Give up! Take a hint! He couldn't make it any clearer if he made you a human cannonball and lit the fuse, giggling*

the whole time! THE GUY DOESN'T LIKE YOU!
FUCK OFF!)

'What the hell's that supposed to mean?' Mark asked.
'I'm exactly like this. That's what being like *this* means.'

The same nasty tone of voice, but for a second a note of
enquiry had entered the equation, like a glimpse of the real
clone of Mark underneath the mask of the real Mark.

'He's worrying about something,' Top Brain said. 'He's
worried and angry and upset, and he's never really been
any of those things before. You have to find out what's
bugging him.'

(*Yeah, you have to take care of him,* Bottom Brain
sneered. *Isn't that sweet?*)

'You're acting like this,' Kirsty said, 'but it isn't who
you really are.'

Mark snorted (it came so naturally!) and said, 'What do
you know about who I really am?'

Kirsty just smiled and shrugged in a way she hoped
came across as understanding.

(*Bullshit, you look like a pretentious bitch who's just
lost an argument.*)

Mark lost interest and walked off, leaving Kirsty
trapped in the swarm of other footballers who were now
coming out of the changing rooms.

For the rest of that lunchtime she prayed. It felt empty
at first, like shaking your fist at a tidal wave, but it had
done before in times of trouble and she'd still got something in return, even if sometimes it was just a case of
'God's not here at the moment, try and solve this one yourself, and if that doesn't work, leave a message after the tone.'

Sometimes she prayed with a request, either a spur of
the moment 'Don't let me be knocked out of rounders' or
a constant 'Give me the strength not to hate those bastards

who make jokes about Bible bashers.' Sometimes she was thankful – 'Thank God I got a good mark in that exam!' – and sometimes she just wanted someone to blame, or to tell the guy upstairs He'd really fucked it up this time. Such as the time He'd let Mark die without giving her so much as a kind word his whole life. That, Kirsty felt, had been entirely unfair, and she'd ranted and raged against Him for days. Later she'd realized she was being selfish and stupid, and had apologized, but like all good friends God was there when you needed to be pissed off at someone, and He didn't take it personally.

This time she prayed for Mark's clone, prayed that God would help her to help him. For a while all she got was the on-hold music of the heavens, but then it hit her. Mark wouldn't open up to her at school, not in front of the prying eyes of his classmates, particularly Phil, who Kirsty suspected he looked to as a role model. She wouldn't be able to talk to him after school either. Mark and Phil always walked home together, and even when the clone had been normal Phil was always hostile, overtly or on the quiet.

No, the time to talk to Mark would be at his house, around fourish, say, after Phil had gone home.

Bottom Brain began to say something, but Kirsty quickly tied it up and gagged it, before kicking it into her own mental cellar, where it writhed and shouted things that she tried to ignore.

'Mark, where are we supposed to be going?'

I'd forgotten my watch and didn't know how long we'd been walking, but it felt like a bloody long time.

'Will you stop complaining?' Mark said. 'It's not like I asked you to come with me.'

'Yes,' I said silently, 'but it's not like that gives me any choice in the matter, is it?'

It didn't look as if he knew where we were going. We'd just carried on from his road, and then the road had split in two, so we'd taken a left, and then a while later we'd come to a footpath, so Mark had decided to take that, and now we were on our sixth field. My legs were beginning to ache, I was hungry and I wanted to go home.

Mark seemed fine. Fine, that is, except for having walked what must have been a couple of miles with no apparent purpose.

'We should be getting back,' I said. 'Your parents will be expecting you home soon. Mine too.'

'Why should we go back just because they *expect* us?' he asked.

It wasn't a question. It was a jab, an insult, confrontation. Or was it? There'd been just the slightest suggestion that the question wasn't rhetorical.

'Because if we don't they'll worry,' I said.

'Yours might. Mine are on worry overload already,' Mark said. 'My sister's dead,' he added, as if I might have forgotten.

'Yes, but I can't go back unless you come with me.'

We'd stopped in the middle of the field. A little bit of the clone I knew was beginning to show now.

'Well, I guess you could phone them,' Mark said, and began walking again.

I followed. What else could I do?

'Why are we doing this?' I asked him when I caught up.

'I've no idea why *you're* doing this,' he said.

'Okay, why are you doing this?'

'Because I don't want to go home yet.'

'Why not?'

'You know why.'

'Maybe,' I said, 'but I still want you to tell me.'

'Why?'

I shrugged. 'I don't know. See if I'm right, I guess.'

'Because everything's all weird at home,' Mark said. 'I feel like I'm suffocating when I'm there.'

I didn't say anything. I couldn't think of anything to say.

'It's stupid. I mean, there's no less air in the house, but I still feel like I can't breathe there.'

'Yeah,' I said.

I felt useless. This was why me and Mark had always laughed off or taken the piss about stuff that worried us. If we didn't we'd end up talking ourselves out of our depth. For no particular reason I found myself thinking about Kirsty. She had all the tact of a T. Rex at a dinner party, always sticking her nose in when you didn't want it, and generally she thought the world would be better if people were just a bit more like *her*, but she would have something to say in a situation like this.

It might not always be the right thing to say, but it was something. It was better than 'Yeah'.

Then there was Mark. The real Mark, I mean, the real clone. He never said the right thing either, or at least, he never said what you wanted to hear. He'd never tried to be anyone's best buddy or confidant, he'd never said that he was there for me, or told me that he understood what I was going through. Hell, he never understood *anything*.

All he ever did was ask questions and questions and more questions. He didn't draw conclusions, he never read anything into what you said, he just listened because he made the fatal assumption that you knew stuff. It didn't cheer you up, but it made you think about things instead of wallowing in them.

In its own warped little way that was better than 'Yeah' as well.

As we walked on in silence my train of thought threw up something else. I hadn't seen Mark cry.

'Mark?' I asked.

He grunted a reply.

'You're upset about your sister, aren't you?'

All Mark did was look at me.

'Sorry, stupid question,' I said. 'It's just, although you've been acting . . . well . . . you've not actually cried. I was just wondering why.'

It was a harsh, tactless question, but I felt I'd earned a few from the clone.

He shrugged before answering. 'I dunno. Never had to before. Not sure how.'

It made sense really. Crying is what we did when we were babies, when we were hungry or tired or bored or had just shat ourselves and were frustrated because we just couldn't make people understand. Mark had practically been born with all the vocabulary he'd ever need. He'd never been lost for words, he was always able to explain what was happening in his head and when he didn't understand he'd ask. Except somebody had told him he couldn't ask questions any more and now, now he was just stuck.

It was my fault.

My first response to this wasn't guilt or despair. It was a

stern reprimand to myself: 'For fuck's sake just sort this mess out. You can feel sorry for yourself later.'

I didn't know how to sort this mess out. All I could do was follow Mark to the ends of the earth and say 'Yeah' while he was talking to himself. What use was that?

'Come on, Mark,' I said. 'Let's go home.'

At the time it seemed like the best thing to do. He needed to get home and stop wandering around worrying himself. Part of me knew that I was lying. Part of me knew I was tired and lost and worst of all I was even getting a bit bored. I wanted the whole outing over and I wanted to *go home*.

Mark stared out over the fields. For a second I thought he looked like the clone again – that look of awe was creeping back on to his face. But then it disappeared like a light switching off, and his eyes glazed over.

'Sod it, might as well,' he said, and we turned back.

Kirsty stayed behind after art to help clean the paintbrushes and palettes. This wasn't unusual – she always stayed behind to help clean up in art. She was nice like that. Sure, Bottom Brain would tell her that this was being a creep and a brown-noser, and most of the kids in her class whispered the same thing (or shouted it at her as she left the building), but Kirsty actually enjoyed cleaning the painting things. There was something relaxing about watching the paint disappear under the tap, and the bright, almost clean plastic come through. Almost clean, because after decades of abuse they had odd grey stains and burn marks all over them.

So she let the other kids make their snide comments and repressed the nastier thoughts in her own head, and lost herself in the sound of running water and the patterns the paint made as it swirled into the plughole.

(*Yeah, but today you're being even more careful than usual, aren't you?*)

She hummed a little tune, something she only did when she was certain everyone else had gone home – doubly so because the tune happened to be a hymn. It was a nice tune that was good for humming.

(*I doubt that palette's been as clean since the Berlin Wall fell.*)

She turned it over and used one of the brushes to scrape off a few stubborn flakes.

'Kirsty?'

She glanced over her shoulder to see Mr Heyworth coming in.

'Haven't you got a home to go to?' He chuckled.

Kirsty sighed. She knew she was putting off the inevitable, but eventually she'd have to either do what she'd decided to do, or give up and go home.

'Yes,' she said solemnly, 'I have.'

Mr Heyworth scratched his head as he watched her leave. What was all that about?

Kirsty felt like she was struggling against a strong wind as she walked towards Mark's house. With every step her heartbeat quickened and Bottom Brain sneered and taunted her further.

She'd only been to Mark's house once before. She'd gone for a walk after school and passed his house as he and Phil were going in.

(*You mean you followed him home.*)

What if she had? It wasn't as if there was a law against it.

(*Actually it's called stalking.*)

Well, her intentions had been good. Okay, she hadn't really had any intentions. She'd left school, decided to go for a walk, had seen Mark and Phil and had just . . . followed them home.

But the point was, the point was that it was all working out for the best. If she hadn't followed Mark home then, she wouldn't know how to get to his house to talk to his clone now.

When she got to the end of his road she sat down for a bit. (*Not that you're scared or anything.*) She checked her watch. It was three minutes past four. Probably too early. Phil might have stayed to play video games or look at porn or whatever it was boys did at each other's houses. She decided to go for a walk round the block, then come back and ring Mark's doorbell.

(*It won't work, you know. You'll get there to find they're eating dinner, or that Phil's still there, or Mark will simply tell you to bugger off.*)

'At least I'll know I've tried,' Kirsty said to herself, not even noticing the words had slipped out of her mouth.

(*Very noble.*)

By twenty-two minutes past four she decided she couldn't put it off any longer. She'd walked round the block twice, been to the corner shop and got a Dr Pepper. She'd drunk the Dr Pepper and now she was stood outside Mark's house, willing herself to push the doorbell. She couldn't lift her arms from her sides, it was as if she was holding bags of heavy shopping.

(*You could go now. You could turn around and walk away and no one need ever know what a complete freak you are. You never have to tell anyone. Just go, now, before someone looks out of the window and sees that dippy redhead standing outside in a hypnotic trance.*)

She lifted her finger.

It stopped, hovering over the doorbell.

(*Run! Run away!*)

She heard a pair of footsteps turn the corner and span round.

It was a young couple. They walked past her without giving her a second glance. They were too busy concentrating on gazing dreamily into each other's eyes and walking the dog. Kirsty watched them to the end of the cul-de-sac and on to the little footpath at the end.

She took a deep breath and turned back to the doorbell.

Then her finger shot up and pushed the button in.

DING.

Her finger was pressed hard against the button so that its tip was red and bending backwards. She pulled it back.

DONG.

She felt her feet freeze into the ground. She held her breath, tensed up completely. She felt as if she'd pulled a trigger instead of pushing a doorbell. People began to move around inside. Through the warping glass of the front door she saw a silhouette move towards the door and heard the click of the latch being taken off.

(*Too late. You should have run.*)

'Hello?'

It was Mark's dad.

'Hello, Mr Self. I'm a friend of Mark's. Could I speak to him?' said Kirsty in her polite-speaking-to-grown-ups voice.

For a moment Mark's dad seemed not to hear. Then he said, 'Mark's not in at the moment. He should be back soon, though. Do you want to come in and wait?'

'Um, sure . . .' Kirsty said, feeling a bit lost.

Mark's dad stood back to let her in, and she stepped through the door to stand in the middle of the hall carpet. She continued to stand there while Mark's dad walked into the front room.

'Come into the front room and take a seat,' Mark's mum said.

Her voice sounded as if it had been stretched over a drum – taut and on the verge of ripping.

Kirsty walked into the front room, but declined the offer of a seat. Then after standing for a couple of minutes she felt stupid, so sat down as quickly as possible. Somewhere a clock was ticking, but she couldn't tell where.

'Would you like a cup of tea or coffee?' Mark's dad asked.

'No, thank you,' Kirsty said automatically.

'Would you like a soft drink or some fruit juice?'

'No, thank you,' Kirsty said again, although her throat was parched.

She gazed at the photographs on the walls, and felt a sense of resentment and curiosity at the wealth of life the old Mark had lived that she knew nothing about.

(*You sound like a stalker . . . but then you have just come into his house under false pretences to corner him on his own, so I suppose that's the least of your worries.*)

False pretences?

(*'Hello, Mr Self. I'm a friend of Mark's.'*)

Oh *that*.

Then she realized something was amiss.

'Where's Lauren?' she asked.

That drop in temperature was imaginary, surely?

'Mark didn't tell you?' Mark's mum choked.

Kirsty could only shake her head.

Mark's dad sighed. 'Lauren died yesterday.'

He said it matter-of-factly, as if he was talking about her being grounded or over at a friend's.

'Denial,' Kirsty thought at once, 'or repression or some macho thing.'

(*Ooh, we have been studying our Trisha, haven't we?*)

'Oh dear,' she said. The words seemed to fall from her mouth like dead fish from a net. She didn't believe in blaspheming, and didn't feel comfortable swearing in front of someone's parents. 'I'm *so* sorry . . .'

Normally she might have congratulated herself on being so sensitive and understanding. This time she didn't. Their daughter had just died and the best she could offer was a half-sincere apology. Fat lot of good that would do. She wanted to leave, she wanted to get up and run out the door and go back to comforting girls who'd been dumped by their boyfriends. But she knew that getting up and running away after someone told you their daughter had died was somehow bad manners.

Then there was the other thing. Lauren dying explained a hell of a lot about the way Mark had been acting that day, and it also meant that he would really need help right now.

(*Go on*, Bottom Brain said, *admit it. That gives you a thrill.*)

Kirsty ignored this. After all, there was nothing wrong with getting a buzz out of helping people, was there?

(*Depends on where you stand on the issue of being a duplicitous cow, I suppose.*)

Then she heard Mark's key in the latch.

'You coming into school tomorrow?' I asked, as Mark put his key in the lock.

'Sure,' Mark said. 'There's sweet FA else to do.'

'Cool,' I said.

The door swung open. I felt myself tense up, as if the atmosphere in the house was leaking out over the doorstep.

'You wanna come in?' Mark asked.

I wasn't sure whether he wanted me to come in because he was scared of being alone with the family, or whether he didn't really want me to but was trying to be polite. That was the thing about the clone's new persona – he was like the old Mark, but the non-verbals were all screwy. The old Mark was never straight about anything, but I could always read between the lines. He'd be saying one thing and the subtitles would pop into my head saying what he really meant.

'No thanks, I'd better be getting back,' I said, and shrugged to show that this meant Jack, that I was going home to stop my dad from nagging, not because being around this new Mark gave me the creeps.

'K, I'll see you tomorrow,' Mark said, shrugging back to show that he didn't care that I was abandoning him here, that he'd be just fine without me.

As he was closing the door I felt a surge of guilt. 'Mark?' I shouted from the bottom of the driveway.

He stopped.

'Tomorrow, if you wanna talk about anything . . . I mean, anything, no matter how stupid it might sound . . . you know you can always talk to me, don't you?'

I felt like one of those wife-beaters who kick the crap out of their wives and then buy them flowers.

'Well, I'm not sure,' Mark said. 'I mean, no matter how

stupid it might sound to me . . . might still go over your head.'

Was that grudging reconciliation or bitter sulkiness? I couldn't tell. The clone was using all the old signals, but now they meant different things. It was like watching your favourite TV show dubbed into Mandarin.

Mark closed the door.

Walking back, I thought about the clone. Damnit, he'd been so like Mark it hurt! Not just the way he looked, but the way he talked, the way he acted, the way he looked at you. He was identical to the kid in the wheelchair who once sneaked into the changing rooms during PE and left all my clothes under the showers. I mean, how? It couldn't just be DNA, could it? Being a sarky git wasn't like going bald or rolling your tongue. Was it?

They're both missing out, part of my brain whispered. One of them missed out on getting beaten up in rugby and making a twat of himself at the school disco, the other missed out on the first fourteen years of his life and being able to cry. I chucked that idea – it was the kind of pseudo-chat-show-psycho-bullshit that Kirsty might come out with. 'Mark and the clone are the same because they both understand what it is to miss out on things.'

I sighed, and the sigh turned into a laugh. 'You don't half think some crap sometimes,' I said to myself.

105

The moment she heard the door open, Kirsty knew she didn't want to be there, that the whole idea of visiting Mark had been a bad one. From where she was sitting she could see a cat-flap in the kitchen, and part of her thought of just ducking behind the settee, crawling across the carpet and slinking out of the cat-flap before Mark saw her.

She'd felt like this when her church youth club had gone to Alton Towers last summer. She'd convinced herself to go on Oblivion, a ride that was little more than a sheer drop into a dark pit. As she got closer to the front of the queue and the screams got louder, her heartbeat sped up, her palms sweated and she thought about bailing out more than once. But she'd promised herself she'd go through with it and the urge to escape was never given any sway. That was until about five seconds after the ride started. As they ascended the track leading to the drop, she panicked, she begged her friends to let her out, she prayed to God for the ride to break down before it was too late and then she was there, hovering over the drop just long enough for her to breathe in and think, 'God, what have I got myself into?'

Now she was on the edge of the drop, and the pause before the plunge lasted only a second, one really long second.

'Hello, Mark,' his mum said, not noticing or choosing to ignore that he was an hour and a half late.

'Hi, Mum,' Mark said from the hall.

The sarcasm had gone from his voice now. In fact he sounded kind of sad.

'You've got a friend visiting,' his mum said.

Kirsty stiffened. She'd even hoped that perhaps Mark's mum had forgotten her altogether and that she'd be allowed to slip out while the family had dinner. There was only one thing for it – to take the plunge.

She stood up.

'Hi, Mark,' she said.

'Hi, Kirsty,' he said.

She'd been expecting outrage or sneering sarcasm or something to try and embarrass and hurt her. Then she realized that nothing like that would be happening, not in front of his mum anyway.

She was already feeling ashamed and embarrassed, but now the feelings got an extra boost, like a good punch on an already painful bruise.

'Shall we go to my room?' Mark asked.

'If you like,' Kirsty said.

'I insist,' he replied.

Once they were in his room Mark pushed the door hard, but slowed it down before it slammed.

'What are you doing here?'

'I thought you could do with a chat,' she said, looking him in the eye, her voice only wavering a little.

'Fine,' Mark said. 'Chat.'

'Okay,' Kirsty started. 'I know about Lauren. I could tell you weren't yourself today, and I think now I know why.'

Mark snorted. 'That was clever of you.'

Kirsty pressed on. 'You need to learn to talk about your feelings, Mark. You can't just keep them bottled up inside you, otherwise they'll keep getting worse and then the only thing you can do is lash out at people.'

Mark's dead stare never changed.

'How do you feel, Kirsty?' he said.

Kirsty choked. 'Pardon?' Her voice practically shrieked.

'How do you feel?'

'This isn't about me,' she said.

'Why not? Why does it always have to be about me? Everyone's always so interested in how I'm doing, that I'm having a proper birthday, that I'm doing well in football, that I'm coping okay with my dead sister. I mean, *Christ*, it's like I'm still in that fucking chair! So come on, Kirsty, let's forget about me, let's talk about *you*.'

Kirsty said nothing. Her own breathing sounded heavy in her ears.

'I'm fine,' she said eventually.

'Are you now?' Mark said, his mouth twitching upwards at the edges.

'Why are you doing this?' Kirsty asked, almost in a whisper.

'Doing what?'

'*Playing* with me.' Her voice cracked and she bit her lip until she regained her composure. She felt like crying. This was even worse than anything the old Mark had done. The old Mark just hurled abuse and sarky comments. Sometimes (and she'd never been sure how much of this was true and how much of it was her kidding herself) she'd even thought the sarky comments were affectionate in their warped little way. Plus there were few insults that couldn't be met with a martyr's smile and a knowing nod.

There was a knock and instantly the door swung open. Mark's mum came in carrying a tray of biscuits and some glasses of cherryade.

'Hello,' she said, smiling. 'I thought I'd bring you a little snack to keep you going.'

'Thanks, Mum,' Mark said, taking his eyes off Kirsty for the first time since they'd sat down.

'Thanks, Mrs Self,' Kirsty said in her polite-talking-to-grown-ups voice.

Mark's mum stood there for a moment, watching the clone. The clone stared at the carpet. 'How was school today, Mark?' she asked.

He was facing away from his mum, so she didn't see his eyes close and his forehead crease up.

'Mark?' she repeated.

'School was fine, Mum,' Mark said, smiling and turning to face her.

'And you're . . . okay?' his mum asked.

Kirsty half expected another outburst but instead Mark got up, walked over and gave her a hug.

'I'm fine, Mum,' he said.

When Mark let go, his mum laughed humourlessly. 'Anyway, you don't want your mum in here, cramping your style, do you? I'll go get the tea on . . .'

She reversed out of the door, reminding Kirsty of a novelty cuckoo clock.

'That was nice of her,' Kirsty said, taking a sip of cherryade.

Mark picked up a Chocolate Hobnob and stared at it. The plate was heaped with them.

'Yes,' he said, without taking his eyes off the Hobnob.

Kirsty felt herself relax a little, enough to start looking at the room. It was covered in football stuff, posters of footballers, the league tables and match timetables. She didn't understand most of it, but she recognized a room of someone who loved football. On closer inspection she noticed something else: all the tables and lists, everywhere there was a date, all the dates stopped at around the time the old Mark had gone into hospital.

Then there was the mess. There were piles of dirty clothes and loose change and old pieces of homework, but somehow the mess didn't seem entirely accidental. There was something very specific about the way it was laid out, as if Mark had found the bedroom a certain way and done his best to preserve everything exactly the way it was. Right down to the underwear poking out from under the bed. This wasn't a bedroom. It was a museum piece.

'I should go,' Kirsty said.

'Yes,' Mark said. 'I think you should.'

He showed her to the door.

'I'm sorry to hear about your sister,' Kirsty said as she got to the door. 'I only talked to her at your party but she seemed like a lovely girl.'

'Don't worry about it,' Mark said. 'She's coming back soon.'

The website didn't have any lesbian pornography.

Laz-r-us-services.com was part of the official website for something called Proteus Associates, which seemed to be a big biotechnology firm. There was writing about labs all over the world involved in the latest genetics research. The labs were all in places like Africa and Asia, because most of Europe and the US had banned the research they were doing.

The company was so big that it had to be split up into smaller companies. One was Proteus Publishing, which sold books about humans being genetically engineered by aliens millions of years ago, and how in the future people would be able to clone bodies and swap their minds between them. Another, called Elysian Fields, sold seeds for genetically engineered fruit and vegetables that would be larger and tastier than normal ones. They also sold semen for specially bred cattle and racehorses.

Normally Mark would have found this site hilarious. He would have saved the address and emailed it to Phil, and they would have had a good laugh about it the next time he came to stay. This time he didn't feel too much like doing that.

Laz-R-Us™ Services.

The top of the screen read:

Welcome Brian Self! (Click <u>here</u> to log in if this isn't your name)

Laz-R-Us™ Services was the company responsible for cloning. One of the services they offered was to clone one parent or another in an infertile couple, providing them with a baby. Another department, called Lassie-R-Us™ Services, offered to clone dead pets.

Another department cloned dead children.

Reflection

Reflection

When I went to Mark's on the day of Lauren's 'return' I couldn't help feeling a sickening sense of *déjà vu*. Things weren't exactly the same as they'd been when I met Mark's clone. It was Saturday not Sunday, and I'd met Mark in early September, when the sun was as bright as a nuclear blast and the shadows had crisp black outlines on the ground. Now it was February. The sky was a mottled grey and there weren't any distinct shadows, just blurred patches of slightly darker shade.

Last time I'd felt a hell of a lot younger. No, that's not true, I didn't feel young – at the time I *thought* I was very mature. Yet when I approached the house I hadn't known what to expect. I hadn't really believed Mark was dead anyway and I was completely unprepared for just how much reality people were willing to ignore so they could believe what they wanted, what they *needed* to believe. I hadn't been scared.

Over the last few weeks I'd seen Mark getting more and more excited about the return of his sister. If I'd matured a little in the last few months, he'd matured a lifetime. On the weekend of his birthday he'd hardly been able to sit still in the car. He'd been glancing over his shoulder, pushing his face against the window to see the scenery passing, trying to take in everything he could. Last week we'd had a school trip. I let him have the window seat, but he spent the trip chatting with me or just leaning against the glass, eyes closed. The scenery had become moving wallpaper.

The only time I ever saw anything of the childish excitement he'd once had was when he was talking about his sister. He was counting down the days in his homework organizer, talking incessantly about the growth-acceleration techniques they were using on the embryo, the Kwik-Learn programme that would give Lauren's clone her memories and vocabulary, and how the clones were being made in the Far East because of the laws banning cloning here.

At night I'd find myself imagining that lab in Taiwan, or Korea or China, wherever. Everything would be bathed in sterile white light, with faceless scientists scattered around in white coats, or all-over clean-suits, tending a giant vat in the middle of the room, the only real colour being the purple-red fluid that filled it. Then the clouds of fluid would clear, only for a second, and allow you to see a half-formed hand, or a face that was strangely familiar . . .

Of course, this image was as close to reality as radio-active movie monsters are to the children of Chernobyl. For a start, the fluid the clone was being grown in was clear, and the vat the clone was grown in would never be transparent; it was kept dark to simulate the womb, only the recorded voices of the clone's family and friends allowed to penetrate it. Plus the Proteus Corporation was cloning between ten and thirty clones at a time and could probably never afford to devote a whole lab to one clone, and besides, until the clones were in a state to begin the Kwik-Learn process they were left in their incubators undisturbed, with no one to watch them but computers and a lone lab technician.

The fact is, real science might be as interesting and even as horrifying as science fiction, but it rarely has as good a special-effects budget. Still, knowing that didn't help me forget the image, which crept into my mind whenever there was space for it.

I was less scared of Lauren's clone than I was of the effect it could have on Mark. Everything came back to that in the end: what effect would it have on Mark? Sometimes I thought that if someone told me the world would be hit by a meteorite, wiping out all life on earth, my first thought would be 'How'll Mark cope with this?'

The way I saw it there were two alternatives, neither of them very nice. Reaction A: Mark sees Lauren's clone, realizes she's nothing like Lauren, has identity crisis and freaks out. Reaction B: Mark sees Lauren's clone, realizes she's nothing like Lauren, follows in mother's footsteps and decides to ignore it and pretend everything's okay.

My money would have been on A. I wasn't sure Mark knew *how* to delude himself, but he'd changed a lot recently, and when it came to things like football and who Mark actually *was*, delusions appeared like zits at puberty.

When I got to the Selfs' front door it was open again. I rang the doorbell anyway.

Mark poked his head round the living-room door, a weird but familiar smile on his face.

'Phil!' he said cheerfully. 'Come in, Lauren's back!'

I was led into the front room, and again there was the feeling of *déjà vu*. This time the first person I saw was Mark's dad sat in the armchair, looking defeated.

'You don't want her back, do you?' I thought. '*You've* realized that cloning Mark was a mistake, but you're going through with it again because it's all your wife's been thinking about, even though you'd rather grieve in peace, even though you're already way into the red from cloning Mark.' I'd seen the bills piling up on the doormat every morning. 'You've still gone and done it again.'

Part of me thought it was heroic of him to do this for his wife, and that he must really love her. Another part of me, the part of me that was more judgemental, that wasn't even talking about Mark's dad, thought it was cowardly, that if he had any guts, and if he truly loved his wife, he'd stand up to her and help her get on with her own life.

Mark's mum was in the kitchen getting drinks and biscuits. It was strange now I thought about it – Mark's mum didn't usually spend this much time in the kitchen. Was she actually *hiding* from the clones?

Mark sat down next to the latest clone, a wide and shallow smile on his face. 'Say hello, Lauren,' he said.

Lauren looked at me. The likeness was incredible. It was so incredible I almost wondered if Lauren's clone wasn't a reincarnation. The looks, the movements, the way she sat, they'd all been replicated perfectly.

She was exactly like Mark's clone had been on his first day.

'Hi, Phil,' she said. 'You're Mark's friend, aren't you?'

'But you don't normally call him Phil,' Mark said. 'You normally call him Fart-face.'

'Hi, Fart-face,' Lauren's clone said.

I could see the future. The Selfs' house, preserved exactly as it was now, only it wasn't the Self family who lived there but four clones doing not quite perfect impressions of them. In fact, it wasn't even the clones that lived there, but the clones of the clones of the Self family. Whenever one died, through accident or disease or old age, another would just plop out in their place. There were no deaths in the Self family, there wasn't any growing up and leaving, there wasn't any change. Just a shrine to a perfect past that no one could remember and that probably never even existed.

'Hi, Lauren,' I said.

'Why do I call him Fart-face?' the clone was already asking.

'It's a sort of funny lie,' the older clone explained.

'Oh. I thought lying was wrong?'

'Well, it is, but only if the other person doesn't know that you're lying. Phil knows that his name isn't Fart-face, so it's all right to tell him that it is.'

'Fuck me, he's actually acting like a big brother,' I thought.

I watched and listened as Mark explained such fundamental concepts as white lies, sarcasm and taking the piss. He explained that there were certain things people didn't like to talk about, but sometimes Lauren liked to talk about them anyway just for the fun of it.

'What's so fun about making people feel uncomfortable?' Lauren's clone asked.

Mark's clone frowned. 'You have to try it out to understand it,' he said.

The doorbell rang and Mark's mum opened it to a small group of ten-year-old girls.

'Ah, you must be Lauren's friends.' Mark's mum smiled.

'Mark,' I said, giving him a nudge. 'Think maybe we'd better leave for a bit. Fancy getting a DVD out?'

The ten-year-olds filed into the room looking at Lauren's clone with expressions of awe, terror and curiosity.

'Sure, why not?' he said, taking his eyes off his sister for the first time that afternoon.

Kirsty had spent the last few weeks trying not to think about Mark.

Every time she found herself wondering how he was getting on, every time she glimpsed him in the corridor or sat near him in assembly, she was reminded of how he'd talked to her in his room, and then she'd feel that big inflatable rock behind her ribcage expand and she couldn't think about anything else. All her thoughts would focus on remembering his exact tone of voice, the look in his eyes, the way each word felt like a punch.

It wasn't as if she didn't have other things to worry about. Abigail, a friend of hers from church, had just had a massive row with her boyfriend and was texting her most nights to moan about it. Kirsty had a modular exam in science to prepare for and a paper round to do every morning. Mark was just a small part of her life that had taken place between lessons, at the lockers or at the double doors and staircases of the school, and it was easy enough to cut that part out.

So she did. Except for Bottom Brain, which was as fickle as it was vicious.

(*Sure. Abandon him. The going got tough, he said some hurtful things, and now you're just going to leave him to it, is that right?*)

Kirsty wasn't even going to argue. She wasn't going to point out that there were some people you couldn't save, because they didn't *want* to be saved. She mentally rapped herself on the knuckles for not realizing it earlier, in fact.

(*You've got all the integrity of a wet sponge cake.*)

And besides, she had other friends who needed her help.

(*Yeah, because Abigail's worries are so terrible, aren't they? After all, it's not as if her and Richard will be back together by the end of the week, is it?*)

But what were friends for? It's not as if you only needed them in life-or-death situations. Sometimes you needed a friend to offer you tissues and sympathy even when your biggest problem was a complete lack of perspective.

That's why she was in the video store on Saturday. Abigail and Kirsty were going to have a girls' night in with unhealthy amounts of chocolate and a DVD with little or no romance in it. The chocolate wasn't a problem, but the video was proving harder. *Bridget Jones: Edge of Reason*, *Moulin Rouge*, *You've Got M@il*, *Shrek 2* . . . they all came down to exactly the sort of boy-meets-girl plot that you shouldn't watch when you've been dumped.

Kirsty barely heard the tinkling of the bell as two new customers walked in. She'd just picked up *Finding Nemo* (it had no romance in it, but it always made her cry), when she caught a glimpse of a familiar head over the shelf and let the DVD case drop to the floor with a clatter.

Mark and Phil both looked up as Kirsty ducked to retrieve the case. She picked it up, but remained squatting, pretending to look at the movies lower down the shelf.

'Hello, Kirsty,' Mark said, poking his head around the shelf.

'Hello, Mark,' Kirsty said.

'Oh, hi, Kirsty,' Phil said, appearing over the top of the shelf.

'How you doing?' Mark said. '*Feeling* all right?'

'I'm okay,' she said. 'How're you? Isn't your sister's clone arriving today?'

'Yes. How'd you know?'

'I . . . heard, that's all.'

'So, what you here for, Kirst?' Phil asked.

'Girls' night in,' Kirsty said, holding up *Finding Nemo* like a passport.

The three stood in silence for a few seconds, as if they were in a movie stand-off. An observer would have found it easy to imagine that each was pointing a gun at the other two.

'So have you met your . . . new sister yet?' Kirsty asked.

'She's fine,' Mark said. 'Exactly like the old sister, in fact. Nothing fake about her.'

'Okay, I was only asking.'

'Yes, you like to do that, don't you?' Mark said.

With a look like that, he didn't need a gun.

'Hey, Kirsty, why don't you pay for your vid and get out of here?' Phil asked nicely.

'I'm not sure I'm getting this one yet,' Kirsty said. 'I think I might stick around to check a couple of the others.'

'*Finding Nemo* looks good. I'd stick with that one,' Phil said slowly, trying to give each word as much weight as he could.

'I'll think about it,' Kirsty said, and walked over to the next shelf as nonchalantly as she could manage.

Phil and Mark moved across to the opposite side of the room, to look at the new releases.

'Jesus, can you believe that bitch?' Mark whispered.

Kirsty didn't hear Phil's reply.

'Why are you staying here?' she asked herself.

Finding Nemo was probably the best choice for her night with Abigail. She obviously wasn't wanted here, so why was she standing here staring at – she picked up the nearest case to see what it was – *Desperately Sexy Housewives*? What was keeping her here?

'You want to show Mark you aren't afraid of him,' part of her answered.

Why? That was easy enough to answer. It was because she was afraid of him. It hurt to admit that. It occurred to her that for the last few weeks she hadn't simply cut Mark out of her life, she'd been hiding from him.

'Oh, shut up, Kirsty,' she said under her breath.

When was she going to learn to keep her nose out of Mark's business? Hell, she barely even liked him any more. Why should she care what happened to him? Why should she try and help him when he didn't want to be helped?

(*Yeah*, Bottom Brain sang out, *I remember that Bible passage, 'Love Thy Neighbour . . . as Long as Thy Neighbour Is a Nice Person.'*)

She grabbed *Finding Nemo*, strolled over to the till, paid her money, then fled.

'What the hell was up with you then?' I asked as soon as we were out of the video store.

'What?' Mark said, a copy of *Batman Begins* tucked under his arm.

'With Kirsty? You really laid into her back there,' I answered.

'She just gets on my nerves.'

'Since when?'

'Since for ever.'

'A few weeks ago you were inviting her to your birthday party.'

We had been walking for a while before he replied, 'Yeah, well, she was annoying then too. All that "I'm good with children" crap nearly made me hurl.'

I could remember that day as if it was yesterday. It was the last time I'd seen Lauren, and one of the last times I'd seen the clone before he'd turned into this ghost.

I stopped him. 'Mark, what the hell's up?' I said. 'You're not like this. You've never laid into anyone like that before. The old Mark used to hate Kirsty as well, but he'd never lay into her unprovoked, not like that.'

'The old Mark?'

I sighed. 'This isn't about Kirsty, is it? It's about Lauren.'

'What?' Mark said. 'That's so dumb I'm shocked even you could come up with it.'

'You've been like this since Lauren died. You've been more sarky, more insulting than ever. Even the old Mark only really had a go at people he thought deserved it. You bring the knives out whenever anyone dares speak to you!'

'Ahh!' Mark said triumphantly. 'But that doesn't make sense now, does it? Because Lauren's back. She's back and she's the same as she was before, so you can hardly say that's why I'm being a bastard, can you?'

I sighed.

'What?' Mark asked.

'Nothing,' I said, feeling like a coward and deserving to.

'What is it?' Mark asked again.

'You think Lauren's *exactly* the same as she was before?'

'Sure she is,' Mark said without hesitating.

Then he asked the question I'd been dreading since I realized Lauren would be cloned. 'Don't you think so?'

The façade vanished – all you could see was the bright, clear-cut image of Mark's clone shining through. He was vulnerable, he was asking for help, and as much as he was a clone of Mark Self, at that second he could also have been a clone of his mum. In an epiphany worthy of Kirsty I saw that I was being given a second chance, that it wasn't just another person being cloned but the whole situation being re-created, so that I could make the same mistake all over again.

I tried to look into Mark's eyes, and realized I couldn't.

I took a deep breath and said, 'No.'

It took more effort than I thought it would. During the pause that followed I had time to look at a garden wall nearby, an old caravan parked in someone's driveway, a piece of chewing gum that had been part of the pavement for decades. Time to look at anything that wasn't on Mark's face.

'Pardon?'

'No, she isn't exactly like Lauren. In every way that matters she's totally different. She's a great lookalike, a doppelganger, a stunt double, but she is not the person we used to know.'

I had to keep going now or I'd fall, like Wile E Coyote when he looked down after running off a cliff.

'What's more, you *know* that she isn't your sister. You just keep telling yourself that she is, because if she isn't then you've lost your sister, and you won't have the time to tell her all the things that you wanted to tell her, or do all the things that you wanted to do with her. Worst of all, if that clone at your house isn't Lauren, then you know it means that you aren't Mark Self.'

I was gasping when I finished, and this time I had to look at Mark's face. His eyes were made of stone.

'Go away,' he said.

'Mark . . .'

'Just . . . go . . . away.'

'Mark, I didn't –'

'Will you listen to me? I don't want to hear it. Bugger off. I don't want to see you again.'

He walked away, and I remained standing in the same spot until he'd gone down the road and round the corner. Then I went home.

When I got home I went to my room to watch *Batman Begins*. I didn't really enjoy it – it wasn't as much fun without Phil there – but I felt that if you'd gone to the trouble of renting a DVD you might as well watch it, and there was nothing else to do. I could have gone downstairs to play with Lauren, I suppose, or even invited her upstairs to watch the DVD with me – her friends had gone home an hour ago (one of them was in tears, but I don't know why) – and she would have liked it, but I didn't feel like spending time with Lauren just then.

That morning I'd wanted to spend all the time in the world with her: she'd seemed special and new and everything else was new to her and helping her with new things made me happier than ever before.

Lauren had never been like that. She was special, but in a different way. She wasn't new, she was familiar, she'd always been there. Things weren't new to her, but dull and annoying. She was rude and obviously didn't like me. She shouted at me all the time and thought I was stupid. But she was never scared of anything.

If she was thinking something, she'd say it, which I once thought was normal, but now I realize that a lot of things – the way people look at you, the way people's voices change when they talk, the way they stand – are often out of tune with the things they're saying. When Lauren died I found I couldn't say what I was thinking either, because it felt like it was all in there struggling to get out, pushing at my chest and burning behind my eyeballs.

If I did let it out, I was scared that it would rip apart everything in its path.

Lauren would have let it.

When I saw Lauren's clone after my argument with Phil, the differences between her and the old Lauren seemed so clear it hurt to be in the same room. Because when I thought about the differences between the two Laurens it led on to other thoughts – big, horrible thoughts that were so bad I couldn't let them take shape. I felt as if my head was filled with black spaces – places where I couldn't let myself wander because these thoughts lived there, brooding and growing in the darkness.

Phil was in one of those spaces now. He'd mentioned those thoughts and even though I knew it wasn't his fault I hated him for it. Except now I couldn't even let myself know why I hated him, so I convinced myself he'd been saying horrible things about my sister (which was half true) and nagging me too much (part of me agreed with him about Kirsty, but that part was in the black spaces as well). I told myself that was why I hated him.

It half worked.

Sometimes it's amazing how little you need people. I'd been hanging around with one Mark or another since I'd started high school, and for the first few days after the argument it seemed like the world had ended. We hadn't stopped being in the same places – we walked to school at the same time, sat next to each other in the form room, queued up for dinner, me behind him, and then we both went and sat behind the art block. We weren't hanging around *together*, you understand. I was just going through my usual routine, and if he happened to be in the same place, well, I wasn't going to leave on *his* account.

Then Mark didn't turn up at the art block after football practice. I reminded myself that I didn't care – I was fine on my own. I also reminded myself that me and the old Mark had fallen out all the time over some really stupid things, and had always made up by the end of the week.

By Thursday I didn't even go to the art block. I wandered round the playground on my own. It was worrying. Without Mark I didn't have anyone to hang out with. He'd been my normality badge, my 'I'm not a loner' licence.

On Friday Mark walked straight past me at form time and went to sit with Chaz and his mates near the front of the class (where the form tutor made them sit). I watched him for a while, laughing and talking with the class thugs. He didn't say anything stupid or out of place. He never asked a silly question. He fitted right in.

It was a couple of weeks before I realized I still didn't have anyone to hang round with – I just wandered round the playground, sometimes people watching, sometimes finding a corner to sit in and wait for the afternoon lessons.

Maybe I should have been worried about Mark. I knew he'd be finding it hard adjusting to the new Lauren. I knew the crap he must have been going through. He was still, one way or another, my best friend. But I didn't care – he didn't make it possible to care. Whenever I saw him he was pissing about with the football crowd, doing impressions of the teachers or, once or twice, the less popular pupils. In fact, when I saw him now I think I hated him a little. He'd forgotten me.

One lunchtime I was sat on my own as usual, staring at my hamburger with malice and fear. I'd been stuck at the back of the queue and this was all that was left when I got to the front.

'I don't like you and you don't like me,' the hamburger seemed to be saying, 'but if we get this over with as quickly as possible I might not dissolve your stomach.'

Then another voice, one not quite so imaginary, broke in.

'You're looking pretty lonely,' Kirsty said, sitting opposite me.

I looked up – I was still holding the hamburger in midair, so that the bread-bun face was smiling at me in place of Kirsty's, its thin brown tongue hanging out of its mouth.

'I've got my burger for company,' I said.

I wasn't lonely. Well, apart from those times when Mark and his friends would charge past me in the corridor without even noticing, but that made me annoyed more than anything. Was I really so sad that I'd only made one friend since primary school?

'You want to talk?' Kirsty asked.

'I want to eat,' I said, then saw the hurt look on the face of the hamburger. 'Go on then. What about?'

'I don't know. Stuff,' she said in a voice that she probably thought was casual. Then she said, 'You've not been hanging round with Mark for a while.'

'Friends grow apart,' I said, putting the hamburger down.

'Yes . . . but there's usually a reason for it.'

I could see what I was in for now. I'd seen it before with Kirsty's projects and should have known better, but then you always do in hindsight. Kirsty was from the school of counselling that could ask you about a problem you hadn't even thought about, and then explore it in such depth that you'd lie awake at night for weeks worrying about it.

'Maybe there is. Maybe I just don't want to talk about it,' I said meaningfully.

Thing is, inviting Kirsty to a conversation is like doing a job for the Mafia. It might start off harmlessly enough, but soon you're dealing with concrete boots and horse heads and there's no way out that doesn't involve hot pokers or kneecapping.

'Fine,' she said, allowing a pause long enough to let me think she was changing the subject. 'Do you know what Mark's up to at the moment?'

'No, why should I? I don't hang round with him any more.'

'You must see him occasionally.'

'He mucks about with those morons from football practice.'

I took a bite from my hamburger – things were *that* bad.

'But, I mean, stuff like that just happens, doesn't it? People grow up and move on. Hell, I can barely remember the names of my friends in primary school,' I added.

'Sure,' she said in her dead-subtle-reverse-psychology voice, 'so why worry about it?'

'I don't know. Maybe because I feel responsible for him,' I said.

Damn, I *knew* she was using reverse psychology and faking disinterest and a load of other cheap and obvious tricks, but for some reason they were working.

'You can't help someone who doesn't want to be helped,' Kirsty said.

I thought about that. How did I know he didn't want to be helped? Maybe not wanting to be helped was the thing Mark needed help with. When it came down to it, wasn't I just trying to get myself off the hook? Had I even *tried* to talk to Mark since he blew up at me?

I didn't know the answer to any of those questions, so I asked Kirsty.

'Stop being so hard on yourself. You've got your own life to lead as well, you know,' she replied.

'Why are you trying so hard to let me off?' I asked.

I wasn't trying to get at her. I was honestly curious. I'd been expecting her to wax lyrical about the Good Samaritan, Loving Thy Neighbour and asking What Jesus Would Do. She looked away, bit her lip, twiddled her thumbs.

'I just think maybe you're being a bit hard on yourself,' she said.

'It's not so long since *you* were being a bit hard on myself,' I answered. 'Why the sudden sympathy?'

Kirsty turned her attention to her feet and didn't answer.

Since I wasn't Phil's friend any more, I started to hang round with the other people at football practice. This was a lot easier than hanging round with Phil, because I didn't really like any of them. They were stupid and rude, and everything they talked about seemed to be about making someone else feel bad. Because I didn't like any of them, I didn't care what they said. When Chaz said, 'You can be a right fucking weirdo sometimes,' it wasn't a funny lie like the ones Phil told, but it didn't matter if Chaz really thought it, because I knew he was a moron.

It seemed the less things mattered the better I felt. For instance, I felt so bad about Phil when I went to football practice the Tuesday after the argument that I didn't care that I was bad at football. I was still rubbish, but it didn't hurt. I was just going through the mechanics of it, and if anyone said anything I could swear at them and forget about it.

Not caring works for just about everything: Phil, football, schoolwork. If you don't care then it doesn't hurt when it goes wrong. After all, when you think about it, is there anything worth caring about? In science we were taught that the universe is so incredibly vast that it takes light billions of years to cross just a tiny part of it. After that lesson I sat in my room flicking the light switch on and off, trying to spot the light flying across the room. The light was too fast for me to see, so the universe must be really big. Then, in personal insight and social skills we learned that there were millions of people starving all over the world, that the rainforests were being cut down and that there were wars all over the place. The teacher never said it outright, but I got the feeling she was trying to make it sound as if all this was our fault and we had to do something about it, 'we' being group 9R. It looked like an impossible task to me, but if you stop caring there isn't a problem. It doesn't affect me, and if the universe is so big, all the wars and famines and rainforests don't make much difference. Don't care and there isn't a problem.

The only time I couldn't not care, when I had to mind, was when I was with my little sister. When I saw her all the not caring in the world couldn't help. Sometimes I'd sit and play with her for hours and couldn't tear myself away and sometimes seeing her hurt so much that I had to lock myself in my room and pretend to do homework. It was weird: although she was a clone of my sister, sometimes I looked at her and felt like I was remembering something, something that didn't really happen or that fell into the black spaces. Sometimes when I saw her I wanted to hug her and run away from her at the same time.

Some things, things I forced myself to forget and ignore, made me hate her. Stupid things that didn't make sense. Like when we sat down to dinner, and had pudding. Mum would bring in the ice-cream bowls, leave them on the table, and Lauren would just pick up the nearest bowl. She used to spend at least a minute or two eyeing up each bowl, trying to work out which had the most ice cream, but now she would just take the nearest without complaint. Every time she did that I lost my appetite.

Against all expectations, most of all my own, Kirsty and me started hanging out regularly. I wouldn't go so far as to say I actually liked her. She could be preachy, arrogant, patronizing, tactless, ignorant, over-familiar and really, really annoying, but when you could get her to shut up she could be okay.

We'd meet up at lunchtime, not because we'd arranged to meet but because neither of us had anyone else to sit with. Kirsty would usually make some half-arsed attempt to offer counselling, but she was beginning to realize it didn't work with me. Then we'd just wander off and end up sitting behind the art block. I felt a bit of a traitor using the same hang-out spot I'd shared with Mark, but force of habit was too strong for that to stop me.

'Jesus, Mark was being a twat last lesson,' I said as we reached the art block one lunch.

Neither Mark nor last lesson had been the subject of conversation, but I'd caught myself wondering how he and Lauren were doing, and insulting him was a decent way of bringing it up.

Kirsty stiffened at the blasphemy, but nodded in agreement. Mark had been a twat last lesson. He'd been a twat in a lot of lessons recently, sometimes quite a funny twat, performing his impressions of the teachers to the whole class, sometimes just a twat, doing his impression of Larry, a quiet kid with a stutter and a lazy eye.

'You ever wish they'd never cloned him?' Kirsty asked.

'What?'

The question startled me, not in itself but in the way she said it. Kirsty was always asking that sort of question, in that forced casual way of hers that meant she would dissect and analyse your answer like a new species of butterfly. This question hadn't sounded like that. It had sounded like the clone's questions used to, like a thought that had fallen out of the mouth.

'Why would I wish that?'

'I don't know,' she said. 'It's just, when he was dead he was frozen the way you remembered him. He couldn't change, couldn't grow up, couldn't grow away from you.'

'What happened to all that stuff about Mark and the clone being different people?' I asked.

'I used to think that,' Kirsty agreed, 'but just look at him. He's got all his old mannerisms, his old sense of humour, the same grin. It's like he's come back from the dead.'

'No, it's not,' I said without thinking.

She looked at me, and when I saw the blank expression on her face I felt sorry for her in a way.

'You never really knew Mark, did you?' I asked.

Kirsty opened her mouth to protest, probably to come up with some mystical understanding that she and Mark had shared that would be made entirely of fairy dust.

'If you did, you would know that whoever that clone's turned into, it isn't the old Mark,' I interrupted.

'They look the same, act the same, probably even think the same –' Kirsty began.

'Not even slightly,' I said.

For the first time since I'd seen the clone, I could remember Mark with digital clarity.

'Mark might have been a sarky bastard, he might even have been cruel from time to time when he thought people deserved it, and that wasn't too rare,' I said, 'but he cared about the people who he thought were important. He would never say it outright, but that made it more valuable in a way. The old Mark telling me to fuck off made me feel better than any soppy crap could've.'

'And the new Mark?' Kirsty asked.

'I suppose I wanted him to be Mark,' I said. 'That's why it never worked out.'

Only I couldn't help thinking: a few months ago, after Mark's death and before the clone turned up, I'd been in the same situation that I was now, hanging round on my own every lunchtime with nowhere to go. Only back then I wouldn't have even talked to Kirsty, let alone hung round with her regularly. I would have ditched her as quickly, if not as harshly, as Mark would have done. Unlike Mark, Kirsty was still the same person, so what had changed?

I was lying on my bed, staring at the league table I had pinned by the door. I was wondering if maybe I should bring it up to date. It wasn't the first time I'd wondered this. Once I'd even tried to fill in one of the match results, but then my handwriting had looked too neat next to the scrawl that had been written in the fields above it. Besides, it had seemed rude somehow. I didn't know how it could be rude to finish filling in your own posters, but even now that one filled-in result stood away from the paper, like a moustache on the Mona Lisa.

I'd been in my bedroom for over an hour. Elsewhere, my parents were shouting again. It had started off simply enough. Mum had bought us fish and chips for tea and Dad had asked if she thought we were made of money. A few months ago that would have confused me, since we weren't made of money – obviously, we were made of bone and muscles and skin and stuff. Now I understood that he was just finding a silly way to say that we couldn't afford fish and chips. The time when it would have confused me seemed a long way away now. It was like I was looking at the old videos we had, or the photographs on the mantel-piece.

The argument had grown and spread, like they often did these days. The chips lay cold and unopened on the kitchen table, while my parents were arguing about massive, vague things that didn't have anything to do with money any more. For a while, after the argument had just got started, Lauren and me squatted by the door and tried to listen. I heard my name, and Lauren's name, and words like 'always', 'everything' and 'this whole mess' seemed to crop up a lot. They both seemed to be doing that thing where they talked in each other's direction without noticing the other person existed.

It had gone something like this (except it was all much more complicated; they said some things without actually saying them and said other things over and over again):

Mum had bought fish and chips.

Dad said we couldn't afford it.

Mum said it was just a little treat.

Dad said we couldn't afford little treats. There were too many bills with the house and the electrics and the cost of the cloning.

Mum said that this was because he hated the children. (I have no idea how she got from what Dad said to this, but she did.)

Dad said this was ridiculous.

Mum said, 'Is it?'

Then it span off into the always and everything part of the argument. I was feeling a bit sick by this time, and when Lauren looked at me, or asked me about part of the argument, the sick feeling got worse, so I went to my bedroom.

The shouting had stopped now, which meant they were either talking quietly or just being silent. Somehow both seemed worse than the shouting. I found myself wishing Phil was there. I didn't know why, I'd almost succeeded in forgetting him, but right then I really wanted to have him around. Maybe that stuff he'd said about not knowing any of the answers was true, but at least then I wouldn't be the only person who didn't know anything. Lauren didn't know anything either, but she seemed to think that *I* knew everything.

A door slammed and my mum's footsteps came down the hall. She knocked on the door and opened it in the same movement. Once she was in the room she seemed to forget why she was there.

'Hello, Mum,' I said. I couldn't think of much else to say.

'This room's a tip,' she said. 'Clean it up.'

She left, slamming the door.

I got off the bed, ready to tidy my room. Except I wasn't sure how. I mean, some bits were easy – socks and pants went in the underwear drawer, empty cans and crisp packets went in the bin, the plate with the mould growing on it went to the kitchen. Then there were other bits, bits that confused me, like the Subbuteo pieces, or the books. I knew books went on the bookshelf, but *where* did they go on the bookshelf? The same thing applied to the videos and CDs.

I'd never seen the room tidy so I didn't know how it was supposed to look when it was tidy. I assumed that before, I must have liked it the way I found it, or maybe I had everything sorted in accordance with some sophisticated but completely logical system. I stared at the room for ages, waiting for the moment when it would all snap into place and I could say 'Aha! The socks are piled in chronological order,' or 'Oh! The old homework is scattered by subject.'

In the end I decided to apply my not-caring method to tidying the room. I just picked up stuff and put it somewhere else, cramming as much as I could into the wardrobe or under the bed. The not-caring method worked, but every time I picked something up I felt a twinge leap up from my gut and I had to look around to see if anyone was watching.

Soon the room was starting to look quite tidy. The only thing I couldn't move were the dark patches on the carpet where piles had been building up for months and the floor had been deprived of sunlight. It looked as if the ghost of the mess was still clinging to the room even when I'd tidied all I could.

I was trying to force a folder full of old football magazines under the bed when I found it. It didn't seem much at first. I was just trying to force the folder past the bedside chest of drawers when I slipped and my elbow bashed its corner.

I yelped and was rubbing my elbow when I noticed the bit of wood at the bottom of the chest of drawers had toppled over, as if it wasn't stuck to anything but placed there to hide the space behind it. I bent down and looked into the dark gap. There were shapes under the bottom drawer.

I slid my hand into the darkness and found a pile of papers that were smooth to the touch, like magazine covers. They were magazine covers. I pulled out a copy of *FHM*, and then another, and then a page three from the *Sun*. There was a whole pile of magazines and newspapers with pictures of women who weren't wearing many clothes.

I put my hand into the gap again, and this time I felt something hard and plastic. I closed my hand and pulled it out. It was a video cassette. It had a sticker on the case, labelled with blue felt tip.

It said, 'To My Clone'.

In the top left-hand corner of the screen was a photo of a perfect baby, playing with a plastic double helix as if it was Lego.

'Due to breakthroughs in the field of in vitro gestation and accelerated growth,' the website explained, 'it is now possible to create a clone with the physical maturity of a child up to fourteen years old.'

It went on to explain how, with a technique known as Kwik-Learn, it was possible to imprint the clone with memories of its friends and family, familiar locations and routines, likes and dislikes and even anecdotes of important life events, so that for all intents and purposes the clone and the DNA donor would be the same person.

'Your dead child could be miraculously resurrected in six to eight weeks!' the website exclaimed.

As Mark read through the site a cloud of dizziness came down between him and reality. His brain struggled to believe it was dreaming. He read on, about the genetic screening that would allow them to remove genes responsible for certain disorders in new clones.

Disorders like Mark's.

He read the ethical policy of the company. It didn't amount to much. They did go so far as to refuse to clone anyone older than fourteen, as the Kwik-Learn programme wouldn't be able to give anyone over that age the 'emotional maturity that develops with adolescence'. They also refused to clone anyone who wasn't immediate family to the client, and they refused to clone suicides. Save that brief nod to morality, they didn't much care what you asked of them. All you needed to do was provide them with hair, blood and cell samples and a cheque for a hideous amount of money.

Mark remembered the plastic tube, barely more than a

finger's width, of red-black liquid. It had looked deep, sec-
retive. His mum had never asked permission to take that
blood – Mark had never suggested consent was necessary.
He'd given it away like tap water, pointless swill that was
easily replaced.

He felt differently now. That was his *swill.*

Reconstruction

Reconstruction

When I answered the door I should have had some kind of intuition. I should have seen the look in his eyes and said, 'Something's wrong, isn't it?' or at least had the common decency to be shocked when he turned up on my doorstep after weeks of not speaking to me. Instead I said, 'Oh, hi. Come in,' and held the door open for him.

Mark walked in, eyes to the ground, shoulders hunched.

At least I was perceptive enough to ask, 'What's up?' But to be honest that was just to make conversation.

Mark walked into the front room, and stopped.

'What's she doing here?' he asked.

I wasn't sure if he was accusing me, or just asking out of curiosity. He'd changed so much it was taking time to readjust.

'Nothing.'

From my tone of voice it sounded like the sort of nothing that usually involves broken windows or hastily concealed cigarettes.

I didn't know what Kirsty was doing there. At the end of the school day I was feeling bored, so I'd just asked Kirsty if she fancied coming round to mine for a bit. She hadn't had anything better to do either and we were just hanging round my house and chatting.

Mark nodded and sat down. He didn't ask how somebody could be doing nothing.

'Mark, what's wrong?' Kirsty asked.

Until then it hadn't occurred to me something was wrong, and I kicked myself for it.

'Nothing,' Mark muttered.

'Mark, you can't lie to us, we know something's up.'

'Nothing's up, okay?' I said.

It was obvious something was wrong, but I didn't want Kirsty to be the one who discovered it. Mark was *my* friend, and if she was picking up on things that I'd been oblivious to, that meant I'd screwed up. When she'd asked if something was wrong I'd seen it straight away, and it had felt like a punch in the face.

'Mark, come on, you can tell us,' Kirsty continued.

'Kirsty, will you stop fucking pestering him! Stop using that psychiatrist's I'm-so-understanding voice, stop poking your nose in and stop saying his fucking name at the beginning of every sentence!'

Kirsty smiled the way she always did, but her face was pale and her voice trembling when she said, 'I'm only trying to help.'

'Well, go and stick the kettle on,' I said.

Mark didn't like tea. I couldn't stand it. In fact Kirsty was the only person my age I'd ever met who drank tea. Still, it would get her out of the way for a few minutes.

She got up and walked out.

'Okay, Mark, what's going on?' I whispered once she was gone.

Mark unzipped his coat and pulled out a video. My hands shook as he passed it to me. I read the label.

'Shit.'

'I'm scared, Phil.'

'Too right you are.'

It wasn't the most useful thing to say, but I was shocked. The stupidity filter between my brain and my mouth, which didn't work well at the best of times, had now totally collapsed.

'Where'd you find it?'

'A hidden compartment under my sock drawer, on top of a pile of magazines,' Mark said.

'Ah. The Porn Hole,' I said sagely. 'Have you watched it?'

'Not yet. I wanted to have you around when I do. Don't know why.'

'I see.'

I looked at the video. I knew Mark, the original, the real Mark. I'd always thought he would have been pissed off about the cloning, but it never occurred to me that he might actually *know*. He'd never said anything, never so much as hinted at it. I felt the same pang of loss I'd felt when I thought about his hobbies. Yet another chunk of my best friend that I'd known nothing about, that was now lost for ever. Except for what was on this videotape.

If Mark had known about the cloning, and had been pissed off about it, what was on that video could destroy the clone. Sure, the clone had heard about his namesake's sharp tongue and foul temper, but he'd never been on the receiving end of it.

'Mark,' I said, trying to keep my voice casual, 'could you go and give Kirsty a hand with the tea, please?'

Kirsty was surprised to find she was angry with Mark for turning up like he did. She and Phil had been getting on really well. Sure, they'd started tolerating each other simply because there was no one else to hang round with, but over the last couple of weeks she'd got to know him and they were beginning to actually enjoy each other's company.

She'd never really had any friends who weren't part of her church groups or kids of friends of her parents. She'd always had trouble getting on with people in school. When they found out she was a Christian, and that being a Christian mattered to her, they'd been scared off. Except that sometimes, just sometimes, when she was feeling a bit low and hadn't got the strength to tell herself otherwise, she wondered if the Christianity thing wasn't just an excuse. Then she wondered if the real reason she had trouble was just because she was very annoying.

Yet Phil seemed to like her. They might even have been friends, if Mark hadn't come along and ruined it all.

She concentrated on making the tea, struggling to swallow the spiky lump in her throat. She ignored the stinging in her eyes.

Now she thought about it, Mark had always been around one way or another. Every lunchtime, if the conversation lulled, Phil would automatically start talking about Mark. Okay, so it was usually to slag him off, but in retrospect, if Phil hated Mark so much, why did he go on about him all the time?

'Phil asked me to come and give you a hand.'

Kirsty looked up and smiled.

'That's nice of him. Do you and Phil take milk and sugar?'

'Neither of us like tea,' Mark said. 'I think I'll get some orange squash.'

Between them they put all the things on to a tray, and then Kirsty carried it into the front room. Phil was just sitting down.

'So,' he said. 'Do you want to watch this video?'

Mark nodded.

'What video?' Kirsty asked.

'This one,' Phil said, holding it up.

Kirsty read the label and understood.

Phil passed the video to Mark, who placed it in the VCR. There was a click as it fell into place. Mark sat down next to Phil and picked up the remote control.

'Maybe I should go,' Kirsty suggested, stepping towards the door.

'You don't have to,' Phil said. 'I'm sorry about what I said earlier. I was kinda pissed off.'

Kirsty hesitated by the door. She knew the mature thing to do would be to leave right now, but she also wanted to stay more than anything. For some reason she really wanted to feel a part of what was going on. Besides, she told herself, they might need her help.

'Okay, I'll stick around,' she said, sitting on the armchair.

The video switched on, and white static filled the screen.

'What's this?' Kirsty asked.

'Maybe the message is hidden somewhere along the tape?' Phil suggested.

Mark fast-forwarded. He continued to fast-forward for the next twenty minutes, until there was a clunking noise and the video ejected itself. Then he put it back in and rewound it. Again, nothing. The three sat in silence.

'Your CD player is pretty close to the Porn Hole,' Phil said. 'Maybe the magnets in the speakers wiped the tape.'

'Maybe,' Mark sighed.

After the video Phil invited Kirsty and me to stay the night. I'm not sure why he invited Kirsty as well – he'd been behaving strangely towards her since I arrived. When I first came in the pair of them were almost acting like friends. Then Phil started behaving as if he hated Kirsty even more than usual and after the video he seemed shy around her. I didn't feel anything about Kirsty.

It was horrible phoning home. My mum answered the phone and gave a little shriek when she heard my voice. Her voice was odd, full of heavy breathing and sniffling sounds.

She got cross when I told her where I was and that I wanted to stay over.

'Mark! Get right back here right now! I want you at home straight away.'

Then Dad took the phone and told me that maybe it would be better if I stayed at Phil's that night.

Then we went to bed.

'What do you think was on the video?' I asked once Kirsty had fallen asleep.

'I don't know,' Phil said. 'What do you think?'

'I'm not sure either,' I said. 'Or at least, I have an idea, but I don't want to let myself know what that idea is because it's so horrible.'

I lay in the darkness, listening to Phil's breathing. There was something comforting about it. The black spaces seemed to disappear, because whatever you said or thought here it wouldn't mean anything tomorrow morning.

'Does it really matter what the video says?' Phil asked.

I hadn't thought of that. From the second I found the video I'd thought that it would be the most important thing I ever saw.

'Why wouldn't it matter?'

'Well,' Phil said, 'you know who you are, don't you? Who really cares who you were, or who you're supposed to be? It doesn't mean anything, does it?'

'Maybe, but it still *feels* important.'

'Yeah, I know,' Phil said. 'I used to feel the same thing about Sadie Goodman.'

The name sparked something off. It was like a little bridge had been built between this sleepover and another that had happened in a world a long time ago, when there weren't as many things to worry about.

'What happened with her?' I asked.

'She's going out with Chaz now. Hadn't you noticed?' Phil laughed.

I laughed as well. I didn't know why we were laughing. It wasn't that funny. If it had been on one of those stand-up comedy shows or a sitcom I wouldn't have even smiled at it, but at that moment it was the funniest thing in the whole world, and it wasn't just Sadie and Chaz that were funny, but also me and Phil and everything that we'd ever done or talked about. It was all so hilarious that I had water leaking out of the edge of my eyes, I was laughing so hard.

'Phil,' I said eventually.

'Yeah?'

'I've missed you, you know.'

When he replied I swear I could *hear* his smile.

'Yeah, I know. I've missed you too.'

At about two in the morning I whispered, 'Mark?'

No answer.

'Mark? Are you awake?'

Nothing except the sound of light snoring.

I slipped out of bed and tiptoed to the door. My heart was beating fast, my palms were sweating and I was holding my breath. In my head I kept telling myself over and over, 'You're being a complete and utter bastard, Phil.'

I got to the living room and rooted around behind the settee cushions. Eventually I found the video and pulled it out.

I fully intended to show him the video. I just wanted to see it first, make sure it was, well, safe. It was fairly new, so it hadn't been too hard to peel the label off and stick it on to the nearest blank while Mark and Kirsty were in the kitchen. After that it was just a question of playing dumb, and Mark had taught me a few lessons in that.

'What are you doing?'

I jumped and span round.

'Jesus Christ, Kirsty! What you doing, creeping up on me like that?'

'I heard you going down the stairs. I was wondering what you were up to,' she said.

'Nothing. I came down to get a snack.'

She glanced at my hand. 'Video cassettes are very high in calories, you know.'

I've got to admit I was impressed despite myself. I'd never thought Kirsty had it in her to be sarcastic.

'Okay, you've caught me,' I said. 'What are you going to do?'

'You were going to watch the video, right?' Kirsty said.

'Yeah, what of it?'

'Well, stick it on then.'

I gawped.

'What, you aren't going to tell me how immoral it is, or go on about Mark's right to know, or insist that we bring Mark down to watch it with us?' I asked.

She shrugged, another distinctly un-Kirsty-like action. 'I'm assuming you've already thought through that.'

To be fair, I hadn't. I'd panicked, switched the videos as soon as I got the chance and decided to worry about the ethics later.

'Course,' I said.

'Well, you know Mark better than anyone, the clone and the original. So I suppose you're the best person to judge.'

I just nodded.

So we put the video on, and sat down to watch.

I found I was glad that Kirsty was there, as we sat in the darkness with the light of the TV screen playing across our faces. Seeing the old Mark after all this time wasn't something I wanted to do alone.

He was smaller than I remembered him, his skin paler, his smile more forced.

'Hey,' he said, wheeling back from the camera. 'I bet this was a surprise.'

He was trying to sound flippant and not bothered, because that's what he always was.

'Then again, maybe not. It's amazing what you can do with technology these days.' He picked up a pile of papers from the table next to him and began to read. 'Your dead child could be miraculously resurrected in six to eight weeks!' He laughed. 'Six to eight weeks! And if beforehand they gave you a faulty model, why worry? You can get a new one shipped in, good as new!'

Mark took another glance at the paper.

'Through an advanced mix of cutting-edge associative treatments, mnemonic hypnotherapy and attachment simulators, the clone will share the memories, aptitudes, tastes and desirable characteristics of its genetic donor . . . You'll have all my desirable characteristics. Ain't that swell?' he said, grinning coldly. 'Just like the Real Thing.'

He kept reading, silently, as if he'd forgotten the camera was there.

'Oh,' he said suddenly, 'but what's this? Dis-claim-er.' Mark looked closely at the page again, before continuing: 'Clients are warned that Laz-R-Us™ Services clones are *not* a literal resurrection of their genetic donor. They are designed to be a close approximation of a much-loved child, sharing memories and desirable traits with their donor. Laz-R-Us™ Services and its parent corporation, Proteus Associates, however, shall accept no responsibility for *deviations* from the donor's behaviour or appearance.'

Mark let out another laugh. 'Not quite like the real thing then,' he said. He shook his head, staring at the paper.

I wondered, briefly, if he'd been crying. I couldn't tell from the TV.

'No,' he said. 'That's not going to happen. I'm not going to be replaced by some walking, talking living doll. You're going to have to find a new donor, I'm afraid, ol' clone of mine. I made this video because . . . because I wanted to leave a record, in case all else failed. I wanted you to know what I thought of you. But you're not going to have my life, you're not going to swim with hammerhead sharks, or drive a limousine into a swimming pool, or spend the school disco trying to talk Phil on to the dance floor. See this?' He jabbed the papers again. 'Says here they can't clone donors who commit suicide, or donors older than fourteen.' And then I swear he looked at *me*, not the camera, not the clone, but *me*. 'I hit fourteen in six months. I *will* hit fourteen in six months.'

When the video stopped I realized I was holding Kirsty's hand, and pulled away quickly.

He was so *real*. Everything was there, the crooked grin, the look in the eyes, the way his shoulders hung. And yet, it wasn't. This wasn't the Mark I hung out with at school, this was the other Mark, the Mark most people had never met, and who I'd come across only a couple of times: once after we'd had four cans of stolen beer, and Mark had looked distant, sad and scared before the puking began; and sometimes when I was staying, and he'd ask questions that he'd laugh off if he realized I'd heard. And I got the weirdest sensation, as if this person had always been there, *pretending* to be the real Mark, every bit as much as the clone did.

'We can't let Mark see this,' I said.

We both turned to the screen, now showing the static from the unrecorded part of the tape.

Mark had been determined not to die before his four-teenth birthday, not to die while he was young enough to be cloned. You could see it there in . . . well, yeah, God damn it, in his *eyes*. In books anybody that determined would have made it; there was always some almost super-natural force of personality that would spur them on until their task was complete. That hadn't happened with Mark. He just gave up. I've got to confess I was a little ashamed of him for that. He'd always seemed so strong.

'Do we have a choice?' Kirsty asked.

'No,' I said. 'Kirsty, what if he knew he wasn't going to make the six months? How far do you think he would have gone to stop that clone? What if he . . .'

I took a deep breath, and stopped. I wasn't going to finish

that sentence. He wouldn't do that. Surely he wouldn't take his life as if it was all his own. He was *my* friend. Part of that life belonged to me. Mark wouldn't have just thrown it away, would he?

'We destroy the video,' I said. 'Chuck it into a skip or something on the way to school. Mark need never know.'

'I heard what you were talking about in the bedroom,' Kirsty said. 'If he doesn't see this he'll keep wondering about it.'

'Fine, then he keeps wondering about it. Better that than this,' I said, pointing to the TV.

'How can you say that?' Kirsty asked. 'I'd have thought that if you'd learned anything over the last few weeks . . .'

I shook my head. 'When I told him the truth about Lauren he hated me for it. The fact is, some people need lies to keep going, and there's nothing wrong with that. Maybe one day he'll grow out of it, but he'll have to do it himself.'

'But this video's the one thing that might help him do that,' Kirsty said. 'If you were a real friend –'

'Don't you dare,' I interrupted her. 'I'm not going through this again. Think about it. If you had one belief, one truth that told you who you were and why you were here, would you really want to know if it was all a lie?'

'I'd want to know the truth,' she said obstinately.

I looked at her, Kirsty who went to church every Sunday, Kirsty who, whenever life got her down, would go on to her knees, put her hands together and talk to somebody nobody else could see. Kirsty who didn't worry about death, because she *knew* what would happen afterwards.

'No,' I said. 'You wouldn't.'

'Mark might hate you if you show him this,' she said. 'But do you think he'd be any more grateful if he found out you'd hidden it from him?'

'Are you going to tell him?' I asked.

Kirsty shook her head.

'Then that's not a problem, is it?'

At school the next day we hung round together, me, Phil and Kirsty. We met up behind the art block and sat around chatting. We didn't talk about the video.

We talked about my parents, and the argument they'd been having the night before. Phil said that everyone's parents argue. If they didn't have a good yell at each other every so often you would just get loads of long nasty silences, and that's when you'd have to start worrying. I'd never thought of my parents' silences as *nasty* exactly, but there was something about them, the way they made you tiptoe around the house trying to breathe as quietly as possible. They might not be nasty, but they weren't much fun either.

Kirsty suggested that the argument had been waiting to happen for a while.

We talked about my sister as well. She was having trouble at school. People kept telling her she was acting differently, and wasn't doing what Lauren was supposed to do. She was no longer friends with Kate either. Lauren's clone had been told that she didn't like Kate.

I was worried about Lauren and wanted to help her, but didn't know how. After a long discussion, we found Kirsty and Phil didn't know either.

Sometimes me and Phil would take the piss out of Kirsty. We didn't mean to and it wasn't entirely nasty, but it happened. The weird thing was that Kirsty was beginning to take the piss right back.

Life seemed okay. The sun was starting to shine more often, and you could almost smell it that day. Even if home life was a mess, school was all right. I could cope with life being like this for a while.

'You seem cheerful,' Phil said as we walked home.

'I am,' I said. 'For some reason I just feel good today.'

'Good.' Phil smiled. 'You know what? I feel pretty good too.'

We let ourselves into my house and got a couple of choc-ices from the kitchen. My mum starts to stock up on them the moment somebody broadcasts good weather.

'Remember last summer when we had that massive water fight in the garden?' I asked.

Phil didn't seem to hear me, but he was gazing out of the french windows, as if the water fight was still going on there.

'It was on May the twenty-fourth, just before I really started to get sick. Lauren and her friends ran in and started spraying us with water pistols they'd bought from Patel's Newsagent. So I came up with the idea of fixing up a hosepipe and we totally soaked them. They started filling up balloons left over from Lauren's birthday party and chucking them at us. Then Mum came back and found the lawn completely trashed, and her sunflower had been snapped in half by the spray from the hosepipe . . .'

'Yeah, I remember,' Phil said, turning back to me. 'It was great. Your mum went nuts. It was almost scary. I had to stay out in the garden with Lauren and her friends clearing it up, freezing our arses off because we were still soaked through, while you went in for a warm bath.'

He smiled. 'Lauren was gutted. She sulked for a week!'

'I'd forgotten that bit,' I admitted, and began to laugh.

'That's really funny!' Then I noticed Lauren was standing in the doorway, watching us.

'Oh, hi, Lauren,' Phil said.

'Hi, Fart-face,' Lauren said absently.

'What's up?' I asked.

'The opposite of down,' Lauren said. 'Why?'

'No, I meant, how are you?' I said, trying to hide my smile.

'Confused, a little bit worried. A bit like I'm dizzy all the time even though I haven't been spinning round,' Lauren said.

Lauren still hadn't worked out what 'How are you?' meant. She didn't realize it didn't actually mean, 'How are you?', it just meant, 'I know you exist.'

'Where were you last night?' Lauren asked.

'Over at Phil's, why?'

'Was Dad there as well?'

I began to realize what Lauren had meant by the dizziness.

'No. Why?'

The water fight vanished. The sun was forgotten. The nice happy feeling I'd been nurturing, the one that feels like having your stomach filled with that gas that makes balloons float, disappeared.

'After you phoned there was more shouting,' Lauren said. 'I couldn't understand much of it, but at the end Dad went out the door and slammed it really loudly. I don't know where he went and Mum won't tell me. Then Mum sat in the front room and cried all night.'

'What's she like now?' Phil asked.

'She's fine,' Lauren said. 'She's been smiling all day. She even let me stay at home all day and she did some colouring in with me, and we had ice cream. But when I ask about

Dad she tells me not to mind and I can't help trying to think where he is.'

'He'll be in touch sooner or later,' Phil said. 'Don't worry about that.'

'But she wants to know where he is *now*,' I pointed out.

Then Mum came in.

'Mark,' she cried, rushing over and putting her arms tight around me so that her perfume filled my nostrils.

I liked that smell. It was one of the first I'd ever smelled and it reminded me of comfort, of things being simple and nice. Except right now that reminder made things worse, made them that bit more muddy and complicated.

'Mark! Don't ever run off again like that without telling us!' Mum was saying, and I could see she was almost crying.

'Sorry, Mum,' I said.

Sorry is another word that doesn't really mean what it's supposed to. I started off thinking that it meant you regretted doing something, that it hurt knowing you'd done something you shouldn't have. Sometimes it does mean that, but most of the time it just means, 'Shut up about it.'

Mum pulled herself away from me and, sniffing slightly, said, 'I've just finished the ironing. Could you and Lauren go and sort out your clothes, please?'

We filed out of the kitchen obediently. Phil was about to follow when Mum said, 'Phil, could you give me a hand with getting the dinner ready?'

So Phil stayed downstairs while Lauren and me went to put our clothes away.

I was shocked when Mark's mum asked me to stick around. Until then I'd felt like a fly on the wall, that I wasn't really part of the drama that was going on and could slip out of the door at any time.

As Mark and Lauren scampered up the stairs, their mum passed me a red pepper and asked me to start chopping it.

'I thought I'd do us a nice curry tonight,' she said, getting a jar out of the cupboard – it was the size of a boxing glove, filled with yellow paste, with CURRY written on the label in ornamental lettering.

'Sounds good,' I agreed.

I put all my concentration into chopping the pepper. I'm not gloating when I say I believe it might have been the most precisely chopped pepper in the entire history of cookery.

'I see you and Mark have made up again,' Mark's mum said eventually.

'Yeah,' I answered, leaning closer to the pepper to make sure the corners of the chunks were perfect right angles.

'I'm so glad. Mark didn't say anything, but I could tell something was wrong. Us mums have a way of knowing these things,' she said, giving me a conspiratorial wink.

'Well, we're getting on much better now,' I said.

I didn't want to have this conversation with Mark's mum. Not again. I didn't want to have *any* conversation with Mark's mum, and it wasn't just because she made me feel uncomfortable. Talking to your friend's parents about your friend is a kind of betrayal.

'He really is his old self now, isn't he?' she continued.

I concentrated on chopping the pepper. I wasn't going to get drawn into this. Lying was cowardly, telling the truth caused trouble, so I was going to keep quiet.

'For a while I was worried that he might turn out to be

completely different, that what I'd done was a mistake, but I can see I made the right choice now . . .'

I didn't stop chopping. I didn't look up.

'If I hadn't, he might have lived six months, maybe even a year, but after that we would have lost him for ever. Now he has years ahead of him . . .'

I stopped.

'. . . and he looked so peaceful. It was like when I used to read him bedtime stories. Yes. I'm glad I did what I did.'

I couldn't chop any more. My hands were shaking. I didn't want to think. I didn't want to hear what she was telling me.

'You killed him,' I whispered. My voice was shaking even more than my hands. Now my whole body was shaking so much I was almost buzzing.

'I'm sorry?' Mark's mum asked, turning to face me. 'I didn't quite catch what you said.'

I was suddenly overcome with anger. It fell on me like a cartoon anvil, striking me dumb. I couldn't believe it, not just what she'd done, but how she was acting about it. I saw her face and *knew* that she would never believe in a million years that she'd done anything wrong. She simply couldn't see. I wanted to punch her, I wanted to punch her so fucking hard she couldn't get up again, but my entire body was locked.

It made sense now. Why she couldn't ever let herself believe that the clone wasn't Mark Self. If he wasn't Mark, then Angela Self would have had to accept that she had murdered her own child. Her brain had gone to great lengths not to let that happen.

I saw all the choices I had. I could have screamed at her, hit her, shouted that she was just so fucking stupid, that she killed my best friend out of sheer *cowardice*. I could have reported her to the police. Angela wasn't a professional murderer and I wouldn't mind betting she'd left a nice healthy trail of evidence. I could have yelled from the rooftops that she was a killer. But I knew that none of it would do any good because she would never be able to see what she had done. There wasn't a punishment available from any justice system in the world that would be worth anything while she was in her little dream world. But what if you could take that dream world away?

I looked at her. She had finished chopping the chicken up and had thrown it into the frying pan. She was being so normal.

'I'm done,' I said, pushing the chopping board across the kitchen table.

'Thanks,' she said cheerfully, adding the peppers to the frying pan.

'I'll go see how Mark and Lauren are getting on,' I said, walking out before she could speak. Before I could punch her in the mouth.

As I passed the bottom of the stairs I grabbed my schoolbag. I put my hand inside and felt the cool plastic case of the video. I'd passed a skip on the way into school and the big bins behind the school kitchen and several more bins on the way back to Mark's, but somehow I'd forgotten to throw the video away.

I found Mark in his room, shoving the last few socks into his drawer.

'Hiya,' I said as normally as I could manage.

'Hi, Phil. Does Mum need any more help?'

'No, I don't think there's anything we can do,' I answered honestly. 'Where's Lauren?'

'She's in her room reading,' Mark said.

I sat down, and took a good look at my friend. He was

a different person, different from the boy in the wheel-chair who I'd tried my first cigarette with and who always knew exactly what to say. Different from the wide-eyed infant I'd met more recently. I suppose in a lot of ways how he'd turned out was down to the things I'd done and said, but, and here's the creepy part, a lot of who *I* was came down to what *he'd* done and said.

I realized I needed him.

'Mark,' I said, 'I've got something in my bag that's going to change a lot of things, but before I show it to you, I want you to know something, okay?'

Mark nodded. 'It's the video, right?'

I blinked and stared.

'Come on, Phil, I'm not totally stupid.'

I allowed myself a small smile. 'I know. But before we watch it I need you to know something. It doesn't matter what it says on here, okay? And even if it does, and even if it changes who you are or who you think you are, what it won't change is that right now you're my best mate, and whatever happens, I'm going to be there to lend a hand, all right?'

Okay, it was mushy crap, but it was true, and I had to say it.

Mark nodded, and I knew he understood.

'I love you, you know.'

Mark grinned. 'Fuck off.'

I grinned right back.

Then we put the video on, and watched it together.

Acknowledgements

I'd like to thank the first people to read *Mark II*: Jacob Robinson, Melissa Garland, Marion Golberg and Megan Farnell. Their friendship, support and constructive abuse have made this a better book, and me a better person.

Also, my mum and dad, for all the obvious reasons and a few slightly less obvious ones.

And finally, Peter Straus, Rowan Routh, Emma Hargrave and Luke Brown, for turning my story into a real live book.